'I am suggest **become Mila's** **Stay,** *bella* **and marry me.'**

Luca knew from the look on Gracie's face that she hadn't seen his suggestion coming any more than he had. But now he had said it aloud, it felt...right.

Her throat worked. 'Luca, you don't mean that.'

He took her by the hands. 'If I didn't mean it I would not have said it. It is a sensible idea. We get along. We both love Mila. I think it is actually an excellent solution.'

Her cheeks warmed so fast and so pink he knew that he had shocked her. He revelled in what that choice would mean in terms of companionship, in terms of Mila's happiness, in terms of having her all to himself, of being able to count on waking up to her warmth and beauty for the rest of his life...

It took a few moments before he noticed her vehemently shaking her head…

Ally Blake worked in retail, danced on television, and acted in friends' short films until the writing bug could no longer be ignored. And, as her mother had read romance novels ever since Ally was a baby, the aspiration to write Mills & Boon® novels had been almost bred into her. Ally married her gorgeous husband Mark in Las Vegas (no Elvis in sight, thank you very much), and they live in beautiful Melbourne, Australia. Her husband cooks, he cleans, and he's the love of her life. How's that for a hero?

Recent books by the same author:

THE WEDDING WISH
MARRIAGE MATERIAL
MARRIAGE MAKE-OVER
HOW TO MARRY A BILLIONAIRE

A MOTHER FOR HIS DAUGHTER

BY
ALLY BLAKE

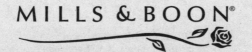

MILLS & BOON®

To Gianni and Christine, for doing such an extraordinary job
in parenting my very own Italian hero.

*First published in Great Britain 2005
Harlequin Mills & Boon Limited,
Eton House, 18-24 Paradise Road, Richmond, Surrey TW9 1SR*

© Ally Blake 2005

ISBN 0 263 84233 9

*Set in Times Roman 10½ on 12 pt.
02-0505-50312*

*Printed and bound in Spain
by Litografia Rosés, S.A., Barcelona*

CHAPTER ONE

GRACIE LANE was in Rome looking for a man. And not just any man. Her father.

Peering into the mystical waters of the Trevi Fountain, she blinked dry, tired eyes. She had half-heartedly thrown one coin already. According to local myth, she would now one day return to the eternal city.

A second coin now warmed her palm. The second coin was the important coin. The second coin was the wish coin. Searching for her father on her own had produced no results and the Australian Embassy had not come back with anything helpful, so a wish seemed to be her only remaining hope.

'I wish to find Antonio Graziano,' Gracie said aloud, hoping with all of her might that somehow this enchanted old fountain would be able to help. She turned, tossed the coin over her left shoulder, and listened for the soft, fateful splash.

But the statue of Neptune looked down on her, benign as he ever was, and unless he had come to life a quarter century before and had a fling with her then nineteen-year-old mother, her last-ditch desperate wish had not produced instant results.

Gracie managed a flickering smile at the thought, even though it meant there was nowhere else to turn. She was down to her last several euros in the bank, she was paid up in her hostel for only one more night, and her wallet held little more than the return train ticket from Termini Station to Leonardo da Vinci Airport. She had very little choice other than to make a phone call to the airline in order to use her open-ended ticket to book a flight home the next day.

She slumped down onto the low concrete wall with her back to the fountain. She was so exhausted her limbs ached, her heart ached, even her hair ached.

But it was not enough to make her cry. The ability had abandoned her. And right when she needed it most. Since that dreaded phone call from her stepfather, she had not cried once. She hadn't had the chance. She had had to be brave for those around her. For her distraught stepfather, for her much younger half-sister and half-brother. For her best friends.

But in Rome she was alone. She didn't have to be brave for anyone but herself, and still she could not enjoy the release that came with a good cry. She covered her face with her hands and willed it to happen.

Success eluded her.

Then she felt a tiny hand clasp her denim-clad knee. Suspecting one of the many beggars prowling the area for spare change and open handbags, Gracie jumped out of her skin. When her backside landed back upon the concrete wall, she found herself face to face not with a beggar but with a little girl in designer clothes.

Gracie rubbed a hand over her aching face and sat up straight. It was like looking at a picture of herself at that age; creamy fair skin, glossy dark curls, serious dark blue eyes, except Gracie had tell-tale Australian freckles across her nose and cheeks. Freckles she had proudly cultivated as a child as they were the one feature that linked her to her lanky blonde, suntanned school friends.

'Hello, sweetie,' she said once she located her voice.

After a brief moment in which the little girl assimilated

the English word, she said, 'Hello,' also in English but with a thick Italian accent. 'My name is Mila.'

'Pleased to meet you, Mila. I'm Gracie.'

Mila was not smiling, or frowning, just watching Gracie with her head tipped to one side. 'Are you OK?'

Gracie cracked an unexpected grin. But there was nothing to be gained from confiding in the little girl. 'Sure, I'm OK. Thank you for asking.'

Gracie looked around for the child's guardian. There were people everywhere, tourists throwing coins, local men selling bottle openers emblazoned with the pope's face, pairs of nuns sifting through the bottle openers, young men 'giving away' one-euro roses.

'Where's your mother?' Gracie asked, taking the little girl by the hand.

'In heaven,' the girl said, her face earnest and calm.

Gracie's gaze snapped back to her cohort. It seemed they had more in common than their looks. 'Well, then, your father? Your...*papa*? Is he here?'

Mila nodded.

'Can you point him out to me?' Gracie asked.

The little girl did not need to. At that moment, Gracie caught sight of a tall male figure moving frantically through the crowd, leaping to see over heads and not caring if he was shoving at people as he went.

Gracie's stomach gave an unexpected little flip. She could tell he was a stunner even with the look of controlled terror on his face. He was immaculately dressed in a black suit and long coat that swished out behind him like a cape as he dodged through the crowd. He had dark hair slightly longer than was fashionable back home, but it looked just right on the tall, dark and handsome types who could be found on many a street corner in Rome.

His eyes flashed so bright she could not make out their colour.

With a brisk shake of her head, Gracie refused to be drawn into the unintentional allurement of the little girl's father. It was the Italian thing, that was all.

Her lifelong captivation with all things Italian had been cemented after she first saw *The Godfather* trilogy. She had watched the films enough times over the years to develop an effusive crush on the charismatic Al Pacino and to be able to repeat entire scenes of dialogue when the opportunity arose. The fact that it had riled her mother to distraction only made the Italian thing more enticing.

'Mi scusi!' Gracie waved one arm madly as she held on tight to her young friend with the other.

'Papa!' Mila called out, imitating Gracie's waving hand.

The sweet, high voice of his daughter was enough to have the man stop, his feet shoulder-width apart, his ears straining to pick up on the familiar sound.

'Call out again,' Gracie said, grabbing Mila about the waist and hitching her up onto her hip.

'Papa. *Vieni qui!'*

The man turned, as though he had extra-sensory radar attuned to that particular voice. He spotted his daughter, his expression went from terror to relief, and he rushed over towards them, in one smooth movement sweeping Mila from Gracie's hip and into his arms, twirling her about, chattering away a million miles a minute in lilting Italian as he went. It was obvious to Gracie's ears that he was chastising her, but it must have been in the most adorable manner, as the little girl would not stop giggling.

Up close and personal, the guy was definite crush material with a good several inches' height advantage over

Mr Pacino, and bone structure that would give Michelangelo's *David* a run for his money.

Once he put Mila down, she started babbling away in Italian and pointing in Gracie's direction. The man bent over, listening intently, before flicking his dark gaze in Gracie's direction.

Melted dark chocolate, she thought as she had her first proper view of the colour of those flashing eyes.

Keeping hold of his daughter's hand, he stood up straight, his tall frame dwarfing her five feet five and a half inches. Now his focus had shifted, Gracie had it one hundred per cent. He looked at her so completely she felt as though he was committing her face to memory. It was riveting. Her stomach flipped a little higher.

Then his mouth flickered with the beginnings of a smile. And, despite the remarkable appeal of his puppy-dog eyes, if she was describing him to the Saturday Night Cocktails gang back home, his smooth, chiselled, perfectly shaped mouth would have been given a litany all on its own.

'Ciao,' he said. His voice was deep and sensuous to Gracie's ears. 'Grazie per—'

Gracie held up her hands and he stopped mid-sentence. She dragged her gaze from that slightly smiling mouth and back to his kind and captivating eyes.

'Whoa. Hang on there, partner. *Non comprende.* Ah, Australian,' she said, pointing to herself. 'I don't *parle* much *Italiano*…' Her words petered out. She found herself shaking her head and flapping her hands and feeling like a madwoman, yet the little girl's father was watching her with an ever-increasing smile lighting his face. His lovely face.

She shook the obscuring thoughts from her head, telling herself that her reaction was a mix of the Italian thing and the relief at having someone looking at her as if she was a real person for the first time in weeks, not just a nuisance with no language skills or a tourist to be taken advantage of.

'Luca Siracusa,' he said, holding out his spare hand.

'Gracie Lane,' she returned, shaking said hand.

He bowed lightly and let her go, but his smiling eyes remained on her. Her hand fluttered to her throat, which was suddenly feeling warm. Mila took a hold of her other hand and swung between the two adults, skipping and dancing and singing some unknown tune to herself.

'You are an Australian, Ms Lane?' Luca asked in perfect English. His accent was lilting and obviously came from American schooling.

'Yep.'

'I'm afraid I mistook you for a Roman. You do not have the same wide-eyed grin of the tourists around here.'

Gracie tried to smile, but her heart was breaking all over again. Of course she looked Italian! That was the problem!

'Well, I am,' she said, still getting used to admitting as much aloud. 'Half, actually.'

'But you don't speak the language?' he asked.

The answer to that was complicated. Too complicated. She waved a dismissive hand and said, 'Only enough to catch a train and buy a piece of pizza.'

That earned her a grin from the guy and any judge would have given her stomach's resultant triple back-flip a perfect ten.

'I was saying how grateful I am that you brought me back my Mila. She is a handful enough within our grounds. I don't know what I was thinking, bringing her here.'

Gracie followed the direction of Luca's sweeping palm

and remembered for the first time since he had happened upon her, all stunningly gorgeous, that she was standing before the just as humbling beauty of the Trevi Fountain.

'You were thinking that you would put a little magic in her day, I expect,' Gracie said. Even in her down-hearted state, its ancient splendour had not gone unnoticed.

Luca's gaze softened, and she felt her cheeks warm nonsensically under his appraisal. 'Hmm,' he said. 'You are right, of course. I do feel Mila should know as much about her homeland as soon as she can. Once she hits her teens I am sure she will turn her back on her culture as so many do these days.'

'She'll watch American TV and wear British clothes,' Gracie agreed. 'I promise that is not just an Italian teen thing. We in Australia call it the cultural cringe.'

'Yes,' he said, with a widening smile that displayed a hint of perfect white teeth within his divine mouth. 'That describes it well.'

'Though what you could possibly cringe from in this country I have no idea,' Gracie said. 'It is the most beautiful place I have ever been.'

'You will not hear me disagreeing. Have you seen much of Italy?'

Gracie shook her head. 'Only Rome.'

She was in Rome with a purpose and sightseeing was the last thing on her mind. Even so, the heavy beauty of the city had worked its magic on her. She knew that at least a small part of her disappointment stemmed from having to leave the city before she had taken the chance to really explore its surrounds.

'Only Rome?' He did not hide his shock, gasping with the dramatic passion Italians lived every second of the day. 'But then you have only seen the tip of the iceberg.

There is so much diverse beauty in our country. You must promise me that you will see some of the countryside.'

It sounded tempting, to be sure. But Gracie had run out of money. And time. And she had more important things on her wish list than to find the perfect villa, vineyard and trattoria.

'I'll try,' she said, covering up her vague promise with an affable smile.

'You are humouring me, I think,' he said.

Gracie was surprised that their language barrier had done nothing to disguise her idle promise. She laughed aloud, for what must have been the first time since arriving on Italian soil, and it felt good. 'I wish I wasn't but I'm afraid I am.'

'Don't think that just because English is my second language I do not understand its nuances.'

Gracie's laughter eased back to a comfortable grin. 'OK. Duly noted.'

He narrowed his eyes. 'You humour me again, do you not?'

Gracie threw out her spare arm. 'Fine. You win. I have no plans to see anything more of your country, as I have no time left in my busy schedule of trapping the locals with my wily English.'

Luca's next smile was warm and enveloping and Gracie felt the odd desire to wrap her arms about herself.

The conversation seemed to have come to a natural end. Gracie felt the moment arrive where she could slip away gracefully. Yet she could not make herself say polite goodbyes. Her tongue would not form the words. She just stood her ground, her gaze lingering on this stranger's lovely, lovely face.

He seemed as disinclined to leave as she was. Then she understood why. He said, 'I am sorry to have to ask, but

I simply must. Mila says you were upset when she found you.'

Gracie blinked in mortification. While she was mentally cataloguing the guy's gorgeous bits, she must have looked a mess with dark rings of exhaustion under her eyes, in her borrowed jacket, dirty shoes and scruffy hair.

'I am all right now,' she said, taking a step back and running her spare hand through her thick curls, hoping to at least make a move towards looking less like a crazy woman.

'But you weren't before. May I ask what is troubling you? I would like to help. Somehow to repay you for helping Mila.'

'No. Thank you. Please, take advantage of this beautiful day and show Mila a good time.'

Gracie blinked as a sudden light mist of spring rain swirled about them. So much for it being a beautiful last day in Rome. Nevertheless…

'The last thing you want her to remember of this day is marking time whilst her dad listened to the ramblings of some self-indulgent stranger.'

Luca looked to his daughter, who was still holding on to each of them, tugging as she chased a pigeon that had strayed too close. But as soon as she reached the limit of their arm reach, she bounded back.

Gracie watched as a slow, wondrous smile grew upon his face. He was in awe of every movement and decision his daughter made. Something deep and lingering twisted painfully inside her.

'She is everything to me,' he said, almost beneath his breath.

It tugged at Gracie's heart. They were both just too perfect. A perfect man and his perfect daughter. And it only managed to hit home what she had missing from her own life, and what she had failed to uncover on her expedition to Rome.

'It was Mila who helped me already. Truly. I should go,' Gracie said, purposely, steadfastly breaking the warm, mesmerising spell that this man and his daughter were unwittingly weaving around her.

Luca looked her way, his devoted smile enduring. And Gracie felt the backs of her eyes pricking uncomfortably with the cruel echo of tears that she knew would never fall.

Gracie blinked to break the tormenting eye contact and crouched down to Mila's eye level. 'Mila, it was lovely to meet you. I think you are very lucky that your *papa* has chosen to show you his favourite places in the city.'

Mila looked up at Luca, her intelligent eyes squinting through the now heavier mist of rain into the bright sunlight. 'Papa loves me very much,' she said as though that explained everything.

Gracie grinned. 'Of course he does. You are a seriously lovable little girl.'

She gave Mila a neat tickle in the ribs, sending her squirming in delight, then stood, extracting herself from the young girl's affectionate grip. 'It was lovely to meet you too, Luca.' She held out her hand.

Luca clasped his spare hand around hers. It was warm and comforting.

'Lovely,' he agreed. And he kept a hold of her hand.

Gracie's eyes flickered up to meet his. There was more than thanks going on behind those eyes. There was unanticipated interest. So, he had felt it too. Pity, since their timing could not have been worse.

Gracie cleared her throat in an effort to dislocate their budding awareness. 'I've kept you from your outing long enough,' she said. Needing a touchstone to ground her,

Gracie pulled her hand away and reached into her jacket pocket for the key to her hostel room.

She found the key, but her wallet, which should have been in the same pocket, was gone. Her eyes wildly scanned the crowds for a furtive figure huddled against the stonework, going through her wallet. But no. The thief was long gone.

It was the last straw. She began to laugh. Loud, uproarious, exhausted laughter turned heads her way. It racked her so hard she had to clutch her stomach to settle the straining muscles within.

Luca watched her in obvious confusion. But it took several moments for Gracie to be able to gather her breath. 'My wallet has been stolen,' she explained.

Luca took her by the arm and did the same wild search for the culprit she had done. 'Please, my family owns a restaurant near by; let me take you to a telephone so you can cancel your credit cards immediately.'

'No,' she said back to him, clasping her hand over his to draw his attention. 'It's OK. All the poor guy would have found is a train ticket, less than one euro in coins, a photo of my friend's scruffy Maltese terrier, Minky, a couple of cappuccino receipts and a video rental card. My *fortune* is stowed back at my hostel.' Her remaining fortune consisting of some laundry that was overdue for a wash.

'Your passport?'

Gracie slapped her thigh. 'Tucked away in a hidden pouch with my airline ticket. Thanks to my clever friend Cara from back home, who expected nothing less from me than having my wallet stolen.'

Gracie's body shook with the last of her dog-tired laughter. Luca took her hand; his palm felt so warm and strong and steady it made her feel suddenly weak in comparison. If she didn't eat, and soon, she would likely not make it back to the hostel.

'I was serious about the restaurant near by,' Luca said, as though reading her mind. 'I was about to take Mila for some lunch. I would be honoured if you would join us as our guest.'

Gracie's mouth dropped open. She was ready to say no; she knew she should say no. She had to get back to the hostel to phone the airline, to call Cara for a lift from the airport when she got back to Melbourne and to scrounge up money from her fellow backpackers for a replacement train ticket. But she was starving. She hadn't had anything more substantial than a cappuccino all day.

'Come with us. Please,' Luca insisted, his voice warm and encouraging, his smile even more so. 'Let me buy you lunch.' He shrugged his coat higher on his shoulders. 'And soon. I fear I am beginning to get rather wet.'

He was right. The rain was coming down harder.

'OK,' she said, looking to the heavens. 'I guess someone else made the decision for me. Thank you.'

Luca nodded, his dark eyes still upon her, and only then did he let go of her arm, his hand slipping away, leaving a tantalising trail of warmth where his sure fingers had been. Mila brought Gracie back to the present by chattering away to her father in staccato Italian.

'Yes,' he answered in English for Gracie's benefit. 'I am hungry too, as is Gracie. So we are going for lunch together.'

'Yippee!' the little girl squealed, pirouetting like a ballerina on the end of her father's hand before pulling him away from the fountain and towards lunch.

As they wound their way through the ever-evolving

crowd, Gracie caught Neptune's eye and thought for one curious moment that he had a smile on his face that had not been there before.

Gracie shook the rain from her navy hooded jacket and Luca from his immaculate black coat as they ran the last few steps into the loud and busy trattoria. Several customers drank their espressos standing at the serving counter, thus saving themselves the exaggerated price of a drink-in coffee, but Luca showed Gracie to a booth deep inside the cosy restaurant.

Pictures of an Italian movie star Gracie could not put a name to lined the walls, and a television tucked high in the corner played the Italian version of an American reality TV show. It only reminded her how disjointed she felt so far from home; everything was at once familiar but just out of reach.

'Your family owns this place?' Gracie asked as Luca helped her remove her utilitarian jacket then hung it over a hook on the wall.

'My late wife's uncle, actually.'

Gracie remembered Mila saying her mother was in heaven and it felt cosmically unfair that the perfect man had lost his perfect wife.

She didn't quite know what to say. She knew what it was like to be on the receiving end of constant sympathy and thus had no intention of bestowing the same. It was half the reason she had come to Italy, to distance herself from the burden relentless pity had brought into her life.

Before Gracie gave in to the overwhelming urge to regurgitate the fairly useless 'there, there', a large man in a tomato-splattered apron hastened to their table carrying a bottle of Chianti and two wine glasses. He placed them on the table before gathering Luca in a bear hug and bubbling away in effusive Italian. Gracie had the feeling they had not seen each other in some time; Luca's cheeks even reddened under the obvious chastisement from the older man.

When he had finished berating Luca, he descended upon Mila, lifting her from the ground and hugging the life out of her. She finally wriggled free of his grasp and tumbled over Luca's knees until she was safely ensconced between her father and the wall.

'Gracie,' Luca said, 'this is Giovanni. Mila's great-uncle. Giovanni, this is Gracie. She is from Australia, though she is half-Italian.' He offered her a wink with his last comment and she could not help but smile.

The elder man blew Gracie an air-kiss and gabbled in Italian. She picked out enough words she recognised to know she was being favourably compared with Venus, the Roman goddess of love.

She tried to hide her snort of laughter behind a measured sip of the undemanding red wine, but Luca was too quick for her.

'You understood *that*, I see. It seems your Italian is selective.'

'Hmm,' Gracie said as Giovanni left with their orders. 'I did the Spanish Steps in my first week here, and I tell you, there I heard some things. The boys who trawl that place could make a packet writing Valentine's Day cards. But, as compliments went, Giovanni's was lovely.'

'And yet not far off the mark,' Luca insisted.

Gracie felt the same unusual warmth envelop her again.

'Please,' Gracie scoffed. She leant her chin on her palm. 'You know what I think it is? Italian men are born with a flattering gene that missed Australian men altogether. Think Romeo. Think Rudy Valentino. Since landing in Rome, I have been approached and asked on a date at least once a day. It's ridiculous. In my tatty old jacket and beanie hat, I am surprised they could even tell I was female!'

Luca's eminently male mouth kicked up at one corner. 'Ah, but that is the thing about we Italians—we have always been able to appreciate a work of art.'

Gracie knew from the twinkle in Luca's eyes that he was baiting her, but her blush insisted on sticking around. 'Please, stop it!' she insisted. Then said, 'But who am I kidding? I don't think you could stop it if you tried. You are flirting machines.'

'You are very pretty,' Mila said to Gracie from out of the blue.

Luca laughed aloud, the sound deep and resonant and utterly infectious. 'See!' he said. 'It's an empirical reality.'

'It's a sickness,' Gracie insisted.

Mila crawled over Luca's lap, rounded the table and plopped herself onto Gracie's lap, making sure the attention of the group was focused back where it belonged. Gracie was thankful; the constant compliments made the snug room feel airless.

Mila's chubby fingers ran down the contours of Gracie's face, the soft pads leaving a tickling trail across her forehead, her nose, her lips and her chin.

'You look like me,' Mila said.

'Do you think so?' Gracie asked, grinning over the young one's head at her father. 'But I have freckles on my nose and you do not.'

'That is true,' Mila said, her face serious as she studied the tiny dots scattered over Gracie's nose. 'I think that means I am prettier than you.'

Luca reached out to scold Mila, but Gracie shushed him

with a blink and a small shake of her head. 'You know what? I think you might be right.'

'Will I look like Gracie when I am as big as her?' Mila asked, bending over backwards to look at Luca. 'Will I too have…freckles? Or will I look like my mother?'

Luca's smile faltered, but only for a second, then it was back in place, extra-bright. He held out his arms and Mila readily scampered back into them, settling on his lap quite happily. 'You will look *just* like your mother, I think.'

Mila looked Gracie over once more then nodded, seeming to find that answer satisfactory. 'OK.'

'She speaks English so well,' Gracie said, aiming to swing the conversation to a less loaded subject.

'We spent several months in England a couple of years ago and she learned to speak both languages at the same time. She spoke a strange hybrid language of her own for some time but it soon sorted itself out. In recent months I fear she has begun to lose the skill, since we have not encouraged it nearly enough at home.'

Luca seemed a million miles away as he ran a hand over his daughter's curls. 'So why have you come to our fair city?' he asked, changing the subject again.

Gracie waited for the usual intense regret to stab through her at the question. But instead she felt a calmness come over her at the thought of confiding in him. Maybe because of the empty glass of wine on the table before her. Maybe because of the remembrance of the impossible smile on Neptune's stone face. Or maybe because of the infinite kindness residing in Luca's deep, dark eyes.

Whatever it was that gave her the courage, she sucked up her apprehension and said, 'I have come to Rome to find my father.'

CHAPTER TWO

'YOUR father is missing?' Luca asked, leaning forward, his voice full of concern.

'Not exactly,' Gracie said. 'I just decided it was time that he was found. He is the Italian part of my half-Italian heritage.'

'And I take it you have not seen him in a long time.'

'Actually never.'

'No!' he cried with that so very Italian fervour that always caught at her. 'A daughter who has never known her father is a sad thing indeed.'

Something akin to wrenching pain slid across the man's expressive eyes, a pain so sharp, so concerned, Gracie felt her own chest constrict in empathy.

Italians and their families were a total astonishment to her. Enzo, the thirty-year-old single guy who ran the hostel she was staying in, still lived with his parents. And his brother, who was long since married, lived in the house next door. Back home, in Melbourne, she went months without catching up with her closest family members but these people couldn't bear to move further than next door. It was so far out of the realm of her experience that she found it hard to grasp. But she was in Italy to try. She had worn herself ragged, grasping with everything she had to discover that which these people took for granted.

'Please, is there any way I can help?' Luca asked.

Gracie was ready to say no. She had been independent for so long, and she had never been one to ask for help.

But everything had felt hopeless only minutes before. Maybe, if there was a time to ask for help, this was it.

'I am sure you are a busy man,' she said, fumbling her way towards a decision.

He shrugged slightly. 'At times. But today is Saturday and Mila and I have no set plans. Do we, Mila?'

Mila shook her head, her curls bouncing back and forth.

'Tell me about it,' he insisted gently.

Gracie baulked, the words *help me* just too unfamiliar to utter. But then she remembered the desperation behind her wish at the fountain, the last-ditch hope she had poured into that coin. What if Luca was the answer to her wish? What if he could lead her to her father? What if he was her last chance to find what she was searching for?

Either way, she had come too far, had burned too many bridges and had exhausted too much of her own spirit not to go the distance. Her mouth twitched with the need to at least try.

Gracie glanced at Mila, who was bouncing up and down in her seat, kicking rhythmically at the table leg.

Luca followed her gaze. 'Mila, why don't you go and see if Zio Giovanni needs a hand?'

Mila's mouth turned down. 'But I don't want to.'

'He might even have some tiramisu for you to nibble on, if you're lucky.'

Mila's eyes grew wide, then without another word she scrambled over her father and raced into the kitchen.

'That's bribery, Dad,' Gracie said with a smile.

'Sometimes you gotta do what you gotta do,' Luca said in an impeccable New York mob accent. If possible, his eyes warmed even more when he smiled.

But there was no use encouraging him. Attraction was a nebulous thing. It was nothing to pin your hopes and dreams on. It came from nowhere and just as easily slid back there. She knew better than most, as she was the result of such an attraction.

'Tell me about your father,' Luca said, splintering the loaded silence.

'All I really have is a name. I know he was about twenty years old and on holiday from law school when he met my mother in Rome twenty-five years ago.'

'Well, there you go. If he is a lawyer, he will be registered.'

'For whatever reason I have not been able to find him that way. Perhaps I have the spelling wrong, or he didn't graduate. With the language barrier it makes it that much more difficult.'

'And your mother cannot give you any more details?' he asked, his voice soft and sensitive.

Gracie flinched as old screaming fights at her mother's house came swimming back. Gracie demanding information and her mother calling her ungrateful and insensitive. Funny; she almost longed for those fights now.

'My mother died several months ago,' Gracie said, playing with the corner of her napkin and rolling her shoulders, holding at bay the incapacitating chill that shot through her every time she remembered. 'But the truth is I never would have come looking for him while she was alive. His very existence was always a sore point for her.'

'I see,' Luca said, the words so loaded she thought he saw a great deal more than she had told him. 'It seems that you are at a crossroads. Ensuring assistance from a local may make all the difference in your quest. So do tell me, what is your father's name?'

The name reverberated around in her head several times before it tripped onto her tongue. She looked down at the table, where her hands rested, pale and cold, upon the chequered tablecloth. 'His name is Antonio Graziano.'

While Gracie looked back up at Luca, her eyes be-seeched him, glittering with desperate hope that perhaps he was the answer to her prayers. Something in her en-gaging face, in her tense body, made Luca truly wish that the name would mean something to him. But unfortu-nately it did not.

'A good, strong name,' he said, knowing his kind words did nothing to heal her disappointment. The anticipation leaked from her body as she shrank back into her chair.

Well, know the man or not, he still owed her. This woman had delivered his Mila back to him in one piece and he had to repay her with more than a hot lunch.

'Like it or not, I am going to help you, Gracie Lane,' he said. The smile that spread across her lovely face was so bright that it dazzled him. He felt it deep down in places that had not made themselves felt in a good long while. It surprised him. She surprised him.

She'd had her wallet stolen and she had laughed! Sarina would have ranted and raved and shouted the piazza down. Mila would have emulated. Bedlam would have ensued, and, as always, he would have had to save the day.

Yet this curiosity before him had laughed. Her day had not needed to be saved. She just went on regardless. And he had been utterly surprised.

Luca had had enough surprises in his life that he thought he had become immune to their effect, but ap-parently he had not. And he quite liked the fact that he was not so impervious after all.

He further surprised himself by pronouncing, 'I...we are heading back home to my villa this afternoon. Why don't you come with us? I have facilities there to help you in your search.'

'No. Thank you but no.' Gracie shook her head, her

dark curls swishing about her ears. Then she shrugged. 'Today is to be my last day in Rome.'

Luca finally understood the full measure of her hopelessness. He knew what hopelessness felt like. For the sake of his family he had beaten it down. But this girl had nobody near and dear to her to help her do that.

'I assume you have an Italian passport, since your father was born here?' His words came as a question.

'I do.'

'Then you can stay in Italy as long as it takes for you to find your father.'

She blinked at him several times. 'Officially, yes. Practically, not a chance. This is it for me. No more time. No more money. No more chances.'

'And if you had the means to stay?'

'Then I would stick around for as long as it took to track him down.' Her voice was measured, her gaze cautious and her top teeth bit down on her lower lip.

It was enough to distract from his burgeoning idea. 'As I said earlier,' he continued, dragging his eyes back to her guarded gaze, 'Mila's language skills have been neglected for far too long. I believe she could benefit from having a live-in English tutor and I would like you to take the position.'

Her mouth popped open and she remained speechless. Before she had the chance to say no, he spelt it out for her. 'You can school Mila in English and in return I will help you find your father.'

There, he thought, *that's an offer she can't refuse.*

'What are you?' she asked. 'My knight in shining armour?'

Luca remembered another time he had been called the same. Once, a few years before, by his younger brother. But where Gracie was looking at him with something akin to awe, his brother's tone had been bitter and accusing. Luca blanked out the image, much preferring to focus on the much more agreeable image before him now.

'Not at all,' he insisted. 'It seems a reasonable bargain to me.'

'But I am not teacher material, Luca,' she said with a hand on her heart. 'I am a casino croupier by trade. I could teach Mila odds. I could teach her how to flip a coin. Heck, I could even teach her to count cards if that tickled your fancy. I have no experience teaching English as a second language.'

Luca was having none of it. She was a stubborn one so he had to try another tack. 'The truth is, Mila has taken to you,' he said.

Gracie flapped a hand in front of her face. 'That's nothing. Kids always gravitate to me. I'm the one who ends up keeping the kids entertained at weddings. Must be the fact that I know many naughty songs.'

Luca could not help but smile. 'Nevertheless, Mila hasn't taken to any strangers in a long while, especially those who threaten to steal my time. It is time for her to let someone new into her social circle, especially since she will be starting school next year. This arrangement would be good for all concerned. It's not personal, Gracie. It's strictly business.'

Gracie watched him with her head cocked on the side, her bright blue eyes clear and her expression open, and then she burst into laughter.

'What's so funny?' Luca asked.

'Do you mean to sound like a character from *The Godfather*, or is *"it's business, not personal"* just another essentially Italian thing?'

Luca had no idea what she was talking about. 'I've never seen the film, sorry.'

'You're kidding me?'

He shook his head and wondered if he had somehow blown it. But her smile only grew. Whatever he had accidentally said, it had worked.

'OK. I'll do it. Your Mila will be speaking like a little Aussie before you know it.'

He released a breath he hadn't realised he was holding. 'Wonderful,' he said, surprised anew at how very much he had hoped she would agree. 'I know I should have asked before even making the offer, but I'm sure you understand I will need some sort of résumé and references.'

Gracie dived into her backpack and after some squirrelling about pulled out a slightly crumpled two-page résumé. She handed it over with a shrug. 'I had it with me today just in case. If I decided to slog it out for another couple of weeks, I would have had to get a job in a pub, or something...'

'Well, Ms Lane,' Luca said after making sure there were a couple of phone numbers he could call, 'it seems that the possible pub has lost out to ''or something''.'

'Papa!' Mila squealed as she bundled back to the table.

Luca grabbed her up as she raced towards them, plonking her onto his lap. He knew he was using her as some sort of shield, a promise to the woman before him that Mila was the only thing between them, though he had a mounting feeling that wasn't entirely true. If he could reunite father and daughter, there was an undeniable symmetry in the idea that he could not ignore.

'Papa, I ate tiramisu and cassata,' his little girl gushed.

'You never did!' he exclaimed, his smile for his daughter easy and true. He gave her a big kiss on the cheek, knowing she would giggle and squeal and love every second of it. 'No, I was mistaken. You taste extra, extra sweet. You must have eaten all those desserts.'

Mila licked her lips, checking how sweet she really was.

'And I have some other good news. Gracie is coming home with us today. Wouldn't you love to introduce her to your *gran-nonna*?'

He watched his daughter carefully for her reaction. Mila looked at him for a few moments as she weighed up the information and he prepared himself for the crying fit that would surely come. She surprised him mightily when she bounced up and down and clapped with all her might.

'Yay! She can meet Pino,' Mila said.

'Your great-grandmother's name is Pino?' Gracie asked, with a twinkle in her eye.

'No!' Mila said with one hand splayed across her mouth in shock. 'My great-grandmother's name is Grannonna. Pino is my horse.'

'Ooh. I see. Well, then, I look forward to meeting both your great-grandmother and your horse. Equally.'

Giovanni arrived back at the table with a tray of fresh pasta and she was surprised at how hungry she was. Famished. But she had been living on pizza and cappuccinos for weeks.

By the time she had finished her generous portion, Luca was barely halfway through his.

'You like pasta, I see,' he said, watching her over his fork.

'You can tell?'

'Aren't there any Italian restaurants in Australia?'

'Tons. Especially in Melbourne. Many even make great pasta but you have to search to find one that makes the pasta fresh and cooks it *al dente*. The food here is unbelievable!' she finished, hoping that would go some way to make up for her ravenous behaviour.

'Good unbelievable, by the looks of your plate. It is so clean you could serve food from it.'

Feeling sassy, Gracie poked out her tongue.

Mila gasped in shock. 'Papa! Did you see what she did?'

Gracie covered her wayward mouth with her napkin.

'I did see,' Luca said, watching Gracie from the corner of his eye.

Great, she thought. *Excellent start. Now he's going to know I wasn't kidding when I said I had no idea how to teach a kid anything except how to mess about.*

Though she had tried to talk Luca out of the arrangement, it genuinely appealed. The chance to stay in Italy alone would have made her day. The chance to do so in a proper house, with proper food, with a bathroom not shared by twenty others and with twenty-four-hour access to a telephone, was beyond her wildest dreams. She just hoped she hadn't blown it with her big mouth and her bad manners.

'What should we do to punish her?' Luca asked Mila, and Gracie held her breath.

'No dessert for Gracie,' Mila suggested without delay.

'Sounds fair to me,' Luca said, and Gracie felt great relief, until Giovanni came out with three plates of dessert and her mouth watered in appreciation of the mounds of multicoloured *gelato*.

'How about I only have one flavour?' Gracie suggested. 'Then you could eat the rest of mine.'

Mila's mouth twisted sideways as she considered the fact that she could come out even further ahead in this new scenario. 'I think that's fair,' she said, nodding sagely. 'As long as you only eat the lemon flavour.'

'Done.'

Mila looked to her father for backing and Gracie did the same. She expected to find him watching Mila with that same rapt amazement that came over him whenever she spoke, but even though he still held his little girl on his lap, his gaze was all on Gracie.

When the guy chose to bestow his attention upon her, he didn't disappoint. Even with a youngster squirming on his lap, he had the ability to make Gracie feel as though she was the only one who held his immediate interest.

Under Luca's encouraging gaze she felt vulnerable, quiet, soft. He had met her at her very worst—her eyes darkened by tired smudges, her hair a mess of ungroomed curls, her spirits downtrodden—and yet he made her feel safe and protected and liked despite it all. So liked she had even eaten a whole bowl of pasta in front of him in two minutes flat!

As though he knew where her thoughts travelled, his perfect sculptured mouth kicked up at the corners and his dark eyes glimmered against his smooth olive skin. Her heart gave a little lurch sideways and she smiled back before delving into her lemon *gelato*.

Only once Mila had finished both desserts did Luca call for his driver. Gracie felt profoundly sad that their delightful meal was over so soon.

'I asked him to meet us at your hostel. I thought we could walk off our lunch first.'

And then Gracie remembered that this meal was just the beginning. She was staying in Italy and could keep looking for her father. The thought took hold. Warming her. Infusing her with hope. Because in finding her father, she had placed a massive amount of hope in finding herself. Only now she had some willing help. She shoved her hands in her pockets to stop herself from reaching out and giving Luca a great big hug.

They said their goodbyes to the effusive Giovanni, and each of the grown-ups took one of Mila's hands. Their pace was slow as they ambled through the winding back streets of Rome. Mila sang and giggled and pointed at interesting things with an outstretched foot, as she was unwilling to let go of either hand.

All evidence of the spring shower had evaporated and the sun seemed to shine more brightly than it had during the rest of her stay. The tourists milling about did not get in her way as she walked by, they seemed excited, enthralled, bewitched.

As Gracie's gaze swept to her right, she took the opportunity to have a good look at the man at her side, the stranger in whom she had placed the remnants of her hope. He could be a psycho killer luring her off to his secluded villa. To torture her before his daughter, his grandmother and horse named Pino? She didn't think so.

'What are you smiling at?' Luca asked.

Gracie looked away, disgusted with herself for having been caught staring. 'Nothing I would dare repeat for fear of being thought a numbskull,' she said.

'*Che cosa è un*…numbskull?' Mila asked.

'Someone who smiles for no good reason at all,' Gracie said.

Once they reached the hostel, Luca and Mila waited outside while Gracie said her goodbyes to Enzo and packed her minimal belongings. Once downstairs she was surprised to see a beautiful black car awaiting her, what with the multitude of tiny dented cars and daredevil motor scooters that trawled the streets of Rome with frightening pace and oblivious to road rules.

The window rolled down and Mila popped out her head. '*Venuto, Gracie!* It's time to go home!'

Home, Gracie thought, taking one last look around the warm stuccoed buildings and cobbled stone streets that championed the history and beauty of Rome, her home for the past few weeks, and she realised that she did not really know what the word *home* meant any more.

Before leaving Melbourne, she had quit her job and sublet her apartment. She was a woman without a home. A woman without a country. A woman without full-blood kin. A woman with her future laid out before her like the paved road below the car, and with her past twinkling back at her like a star just beyond reach of her fingertips. And all she could do to join the two was to take this sudden divergence in her journey.

She took in a deep breath and hopped in the car. They took off, Luca, Mila and she in the back, a driver hidden behind a dark petition. Gracie watched city roads turn into country roads as Rome gave way to the green, undulating Tuscan landscape, with its scattered farmhouses and hilltop villages, and for the first time in a long time she felt as if it could all really happen to her. All she could do was go with the flow and wait and see.

CHAPTER THREE

IT WAS early evening when they reached Luca's Tuscan villa, and it was like something out of a postcard. A long driveway lined with tall, tapered cedars wound up a gently surging hillside covered on the front side by a small private vineyard. At the top of the hill, a sprawling two-storeyed stuccoed farmhouse with an orange tiled roof and an adjacent matching cottage glowed a deep yellow as it soaked in the warmth and light of the setting sun.

'You like?' Luca asked.

'How could I not?' Gracie said on a sigh.

'It's isolated,' he said, and Gracie thought she heard a tinge of…something in his voice.

She pulled her head in from the window and faced him but his gaze remained on the house. 'Rubbish,' she scoffed, and he spun to face her, just as she had intended. 'You know nothing about being isolated. To get here from Melbourne I had to take two separate planes, and was in the air for a total of twenty-four hours. A two-hour drive from Rome is nothing, buddy.'

She had desired to see him relax and she succeeded, though she could have done without the tummy turn that came from one dose of those crinkling eyes.

'I see your point,' he said.

'Besides, the world gets smaller every day. What with the internet and cable TV, nowhere is really isolated any more.'

His dark eyes looked through her, trying to determine

if she was teasing him. 'So they tell me,' he finally said, a cheek crease adding impact to the yummy eye crinkles.

Flushed and flustered by her responses to the man's charming smiles, Gracie stuck her head back out the window, drinking in the cool fresh air. The villa looked quaint, and particular to the region. She would not have been surprised if Luca informed her they still sent post via messengers on horseback.

'You may have access to all means of communication I have at my disposal while you are here, Gracie. *Mi casa, su casa,*' he assured her, and she found it disconcerting but at the same time kind of fabulous that he seemed able to read her thoughts.

Once in front of the house, the tyres crunched to a halt on the gravel. They were met by a number of household staff and a huge black dog tumbled from the large front door and down the ten steps to the driveway.

The humans babbled in Italian over the top of one another, and the big black dog bundled straight up to Luca, throwing itself at him until his paws rested on his chest. Luca ruffled him about the ears yet didn't break conversational stride with his staff for a moment.

Gracie half expected Mila to be bundled up in the arms of a nanny but none came. She remained resolutely attached to her father's side, rubbing the dog's tummy.

Finally, Gracie's host turned to her. He made quite a picture with his pretty daughter standing silently at one side and his large black dog sitting on the other.

'My staff have been apprised as to your role here. I will let you acquaint yourself with them as you go. And this,' Luca ruffled the massive dog's ear, 'is Caesar.'

Caesar greeted Gracie with a loud woof that she felt from head to toe. She waved back, happy to keep her distance, her only real experience with dogs being her friend Kelly's cuddle-sized Maltese terrier.

'What is he?' she asked.

'He's a Newfoundland.'

'Are you sure? I could have sworn he was a bear.'

Mila giggled. 'There are no bears in Tuscany. There are wild boars. But no bears.'

'Great,' Gracie said, suddenly wishing herself back in Australia, where one could find the deadliest snakes and spiders in the world but where the chances of meeting a wild boar in your back yard were slim to none.

'And where is Gran-nonna?' Gracie asked, her voice thin.

Luca cut a glance to the cottage, which stood several metres to the right of the house. 'She lives next door. I am sure you will meet her soon.' He held out an arm. 'For now, please, follow Cat; she will show you to your room.'

Gracie nodded. Amongst the gaggle of staff, a young woman bowed her head and Gracie figured she was Cat.

'*Venuto,*' the girl said. 'Come.'

Gracie's backpack was already being moved off in another direction by one of the men so she had little choice but to *venuto* as ordered.

Inside the house was even more beautiful than on the outside. It was elegant yet comfortable, though it did not show any of the usual evidence that a four-year-old was in residence. Gracie remembered when her half-brother and half-sister were young; their house had been strewn with toy trucks and dolls, with board-game tokens taking up pride of place on side-tables alongside the more adult bric-à-brac. Luca's grounds, with their sprawling vineyard, had promised a working home, but the inside looked more like something out of *Architectural Digest*.

Gracie followed Cat up a large staircase to her room, which turned out to be a small suite with a queen-sized canopy bed, a sitting room by curtained French windows and an *en suite*. The room smelt like freshly laundered sheets and was twice the size of her room in her hostel, which had slept eight snoring backpackers who were mostly into double-figure days of wearing the same unwashed clothes.

She whistled a steady stream of air. 'Jeepers creepers.'

Cat looked to her in confusion but Gracie just smiled and gave her two-thumbs-up, the international sign that all was good. Cat looked relieved and sent Gracie her own tentative two-thumbs-up to show she understood, and then she left, closing the door behind her.

Gracie sat on her bed and waited, having no idea what was expected of her. Five minutes of waiting was all she could take. There was no telephone in her room, and, itching to hear from the Australian Embassy, she went in search of one, or a messenger on horseback; whatever was available.

Besides, it was Saturday night. Kelly and Cara would be on the next plane over if she didn't contact them soon. But for the first time in…forever, she didn't feel like confiding in them. In saying aloud, to them, to those who cared for her, that she still hadn't found her dad.

At least with Luca it was new and fresh, not feeling as if she had to explain herself all over again to the same people. People who loved her, people who would have come over to help her if she had let them, but people who had their lives so together it hurt Gracie to think about them. And it hurt that it hurt her to think about them.

She would call the embassy then go to bed. It was already Sunday morning in Australia, so she had technically missed Saturday Night Cocktails anyway. The girls could wait until the next day, or maybe the next week, when hopefully she would have something of consequence to say.

Once downstairs, Gracie heard Luca's voice. He was having a one-sided conversation behind a half-closed door. She sidled up to the door and listened. It hardly helped she only recognised one word in ten, and none of those words were 'Antonio' or 'Graziano'. Nevertheless, she could not help peeking around the corner.

Luca was seated behind a grand wooden desk, which accommodated a computer, a fax machine and a photocopier.

Gracie realised she had no idea what the guy did for a crust, but by the look of his home, and the state-of-the-art office set-up, whatever it was he earned a pretty penny. No wonder he could afford to hire help on a whim. But she wasn't really hired, was she? They were doing each other a favour.

A sweet gurgle caught her attention. Mila was sitting on a rug on the floor with a doll and a toy palomino horse having a conversation in her lap. The great Caesar lay behind her, and she leaned against his immense bulk.

Gracie could tell Luca was not happy with whoever was on the other end of the phone but he was keeping his voice down for his daughter's sake. His daughter, who it seemed went nowhere but at her father's side.

A warm glow threatened to overcome her. They looked like something out of an advertisement. Father, daughter, warmth, wealth. The perfect family, except for one thing—the missing mother.

Gracie wondered what she had been like, the woman who had managed to land such an exquisite man and produce such a gorgeous little girl. She must have been something else. She must have been sorely missed. And she would be darned difficult to replace.

'*Buonjourno,*' a gravelly voice called from behind Gracie.

'Jeepers creepers!' Gracie shouted, spinning so fast she slammed against the outer wall with a thud.

A tall woman dressed in head-to-toe black, with silver hair dragged back into a low bun, looked down her glorious Roman nose. This had to be Luca's grandmother, Mila's great-grandmother. She had the same elegant height, the same aristocratic cheekbones and the same intelligent brown eyes as her grandson.

'So you are the new English tutor,' the woman said in proud, thickly accented English, obviously awaiting a more dignified response to her arrival than *jeepers creepers*.

'That's me,' Gracie returned brightly. 'And you just have to be…Mila's *gran-nonna*.' She had had to pause so as not to name the woman Pino, after Mila's horse.

Gracie waited for the utterly sensible questions that would surely come next:

Who were her family? That she barely knew.

Where had she worked previously? Croupier in the high-rollers room of Crown Casino in Melbourne, Australia.

Main duties? Fending off wandering hands and marriage proposals from oil barons and visiting billionaires.

Gracie knew that her answers would not have made her past a first interview for such a position in any good home. But Gran-nonna said not another word, so Gracie nodded and filled the silence ably.

'English tutor extraordinaire,' she gabbled. 'Here for Mila. To teach her to talk like a right little Aussie.'

The longer she went the less she could stop the verbal

incontinence. It was as though she was determined to frighten the stern look from the older lady's face. But she was shocked to her little cotton socks when it worked.

A cheeky glimmer lit the old lady's dark brown eyes. 'Good,' Gran-nonna said. 'Our little Mila needs someone with your...skills around here. As does Luca.' Before Gracie could work her way through that cryptic statement Gran-nonna went on, 'You see, our Luca was once a lion.'

Gracie gave her a tight smile, having no idea what one could say to such a statement. 'A lion, you say?'

Gran-nonna sent her a sideways smile as though she knew she was being humoured. These Siracusas were too smart for their own good.

'He was the king of the business world,' the elder lady went on regardless. 'A workaholic, determined to keep the villa flourishing and his mortgage business booming. He thrived on success. Even starting up offices in London. Only when Sarina died did he take a step back. That day he removed himself from the seat of power in his company and devoted all of his time to Mila.'

Gracie was completely enthralled by the older lady's unsolicited spray of information. She listened for and heard the continued clacking of computer keys. 'You mean he hasn't worked in a year?'

The old woman shook her head. 'He works, but he has not once been into the office. They send reports, which he dutifully reads and sends back with comments, but only late into the night once Mila is asleep. During her waking hours, he is at her beck and call.'

Picturing Mila cooing away on the rug, Gracie believed it. 'Luca brought me here to give Mila *my* waking hours instead. Is that what you mean by him needing my skills?'

Gran-nonna said nothing and Gracie was pretty sure the older lady was turning her in knots entirely on purpose.

'He seems to be doing OK working from home,' Gracie said, probing.

Gran-nonna shrugged. 'He fits in as well in the country as he does in the city. His youthful dream was to set up a lost-dogs home on the property until his grades meant that he was sentenced to a working life in town.' Gran-nonna zeroed in on Gracie with such intensity she lost her breath. 'He often brought strays home as a child too.'

Gracie felt her cheeks bake under Gran-nonna's stare, which had all of the concentration of Luca's but not much of the warmth.

Gracie knew that the cover story of her being nothing more than a tutor had not washed with this smart lady. She sent the woman an understanding smile, giving the old lady as good as she got. 'I guess I am no surprise, then?'

After a few moments of silent contemplation Gran-nonna said, 'Oh, I don't know about that, dear. I'm quite hoping that you will be the first of many new surprises. This family is in danger of complacence, and needs a shake-up every few years, and the time for one is long overdue.'

And with that, she walked away. A smile, a nod, a cryptic response or two and off she went, leaving Gracie feeling completely outwitted.

Gracie tripped when the door opened against her shoulder. She moved out of the way to find Luca looking at her in puzzlement.

'Did I just hear Nonna?' he asked, taking a hold of her shoulder as he looked around her.

'That you did,' Gracie said. She was pretty sure that the word that flew from his mouth was not one he would want her teaching Mila, and she quite enjoyed the fact that he wasn't such a perfect gentleman after all.

'Don't sweat it, Luca. I think she kinda liked me.'

Luca let her go just as naturally as he had taken a hold. He blinked, his gaze zeroing in on her fully. 'And what makes you think so?'

'Women have instincts about these things. We can tell if someone likes us or not pretty much instantly.'

Luca shifted until he was leaning against the doorway, his hands disappeared into his trouser pockets and he crossed his ankles. He relaxed and gave her every lick of his attention. 'Can you now?'

Gracie wrung her hands together and rocked back and forth on her toes. 'Mmm. Yep. Uh-huh.'

Silence fell between them. The steady tick-tock of a grandfather clock in the hallway was their only companion.

After several moments, Luca ran a hand over his face, his fingers massaging around his eyes, as though trying to rub some life into his tired skin. 'Well, I am glad. And is everything OK? Are your accommodations suitable?'

'They're lovely. Thank you. I am apparently in the "Blue Room". Pretty swish. In my apartment back home there's the small room or the even smaller room. I had never thought to differentiate by colour. Maybe that would have made all the difference. Perhaps I could have charged more for flatmates if I had.'

The silence returned, though it felt altered. It felt cosier.

'Would you like dinner?' Luca asked, his voice likewise softer and more intimate. 'Cat could prepare you a dish.'

Gracie held a hand to her tummy. 'Still full. But thanks. Anyway, it's a big day tomorrow, my first day of school and all. I think I am going to spend an hour in the shower, washing away the lingering scent of hostel bedding, and rediscovering skin beneath all this grime.'

Luca smiled indulgently and Gracie had to measure her breathing.

'I noticed Mila was with you,' she said, not yet ready to leave, even with her very own shower beckoning her. 'Would you prefer if I took her to bed so you can get some work done?' She took a step inside the doorway to find Mila asleep on the couch, thumb in her mouth. Caesar was snoring on the rug. 'Or I could take Caesar for a walk.'

Luca followed her gaze and she glanced up to find a smile lifting his tempting lips. 'That won't be necessary. He has the run of the place and exercises himself into a deep sleep every day.'

Thank goodness! Gracie thought, and she could feel Luca's knowing laughter though no sound had been made. She flicked a glance his way before focusing on his less vexing daughter. 'Do you want me to take her to bed?'

Luca shook his head. 'No, thanks. It is one of my greatest pleasures, seeing her sleep peacefully.'

By the strength of his statement, Gracie had the feeling peaceful sleep was not something he experienced for himself. No wonder, if he was looking after his daughter all day, running a business by night, as well as looking after the welfare of household staff and an ageing grandmother. Now she had been thrown into the mix she would do all she could to ease his burden. Because the more time he had for himself, the more time he had to help her find her father.

They looked to one another again and their eyes locked. Even in the low lighting, she could feel the zing of awareness, but she was not sure if she was doing the sending or receiving. Either way it was time for bed. Alone!

Gracie backed out into the relative safety of the hallway. 'Great. Groovy. Cool bananas. I'll leave you to it. Sleep tight and I'll see the two of you tomorrow.'

'Buona notte, Gracie,' Luca said, still leaning at his post in the doorway. 'Sleep well.'

Gracie cocked both hands like a pair of pistols then turned and walked away, feeling his dark, knowing eyes burning a pair of holes into her back all the way.

Only once she had reached her room did she remember she had gone in search of a phone and instead had found herself with more than a bit of a crush on her housemate.

Sunday morning Gracie awoke to a view of sunshine streaming through a set of French windows. She stretched her sleepy limbs, the feel of expensive cotton sheets slithering along her arms too good to pass up. Then she sat up with a start.

'Where am I?' she asked the blue wallpaper. When it didn't answer back, she closed her eyes and squeezed her brain until it all tumbled into place. Luca. Mila. English tutor. Last chance to find her dad.

'Alrighty, then.'

Gracie slipped out of the massive canopy bed, feeling just a tad out of her element in her favourite brown T-shirt with *Chocoholics Anonymous* emblazoned across the front, oddly matching leopard-print underpants and utterly mismatched pink bed socks which had seen better days. She padded over to the window, her eyes slits as she squinted against the disgustingly bright sunshine.

Yawning, she yanked open the French windows and padded outside onto a large concrete balcony. Something a heck of a lot more descriptive than *jeepers creepers* shot from her mouth at the view before her.

At the rear of the villa, a large rectangular lawn led to a set of slim stone steps. From there a sand pathway on the left meandered to wooden stables big enough to house several horses. A dressage ring took pride of place in the far centre. And on the right a jade-green creek split acres of natural woodland that crawled up a massive hill, dwarfing the smaller hill on which the house resided.

Gracie leant her elbows against the cool concrete columned wall, closed her eyes and let her face be warmed by the weak spring sunshine that had managed to peek out between the slow-travelling clouds. *'Bello,'* she whispered on a contented sigh.

Only moments later she was roused from her reverie by the scuffle of claws on concrete to her right. She spun about, shocked to find Luca striding towards her with Caesar at his heels. It seemed her balcony was not as private as she had assumed. In fact it ran, unobstructed, the entire length of the upper floor.

'Isn't it beautiful?' Luca asked, seeming not to notice her insufficient attire. He, of course, looked faultless, decked out as he was in black trousers and a black cashmere sweater, the arms pushed up to his elbows.

Gracie grabbed the front of her baggy T-shirt and dragged it as low as could be to cover the tops of her bare legs, but, as she was trying to keep Caesar from snuffling at her feet at the same time, it was fairly difficult.

Once he was within a couple of metres, Luca stopped and leant against the balustrade and looked out over his land, giving Gracie some respite from her struggle to cover herself.

'There is a lot of land for this big lug at least,' he said, looking down at Caesar so Gracie had to do her contortionist act again. 'Is he bothering you?'

'No. Not really. But he is about twenty times the size of the only dog I have ever been this intimately acquainted with.' Gracie had Caesar by the snout as she tried to disentangle his teeth from the bottom of her T-shirt, where a small chocolate stain had garnered his rapt attention.

Thankfully, after one brisk whistle from his master, Caesar dutifully upped and seated himself at Luca's right and Luca once more looked out upon his land rather than towards her bare, goose-pimply legs.

'My grandfather bought this land as a wedding gift for Gran-nonna. He was that certain he was not worthy of her he openly tried to buy her love. He initially received a slap for his efforts, but she did not reject the offer, deciding in the end, quite sensibly, to accept both him and his land. He built the house and the cottage in which Gran-nonna lives today and we restored this monstrosity to its current state several years ago when my business took off.'

Luca turned and shot Gracie a lopsided smile. She did not think for a second that he seriously considered his large home to be a 'monstrosity'. He loved the place. Like him, it was big, strong and beautiful, and brought alive by his family.

Gracie returned his smile though her mind was fast spinning to find a way to casually extricate herself, her bare legs and her fanciful musings from the conversation. Luca on the other hand didn't seem the least concerned by her semi-clad state.

It was probably another Italian thing. Italian sensibilities were very different from Australian ones. Or perhaps it was just a Luca thing. Maybe he often had women in underwear hanging about on his balcony. Or perhaps he just didn't think of her in *that* way after all. Maybe he had simply pigeonholed her as a tutor to his daughter and nothing more. Hmm. Neither of those concepts made her feel any more comfortable. Whatever his reason for being blasé, Gracie was not so enlightened, and wanted to get out of there.

'What time is it?' she asked.

Luca looked to Gracie's bare left arm. She immediately flapped it about in the air to draw his attention upwards. 'Don't even own a watch. Always wanted to, just never found the perfect one.'

Luca watched her for a long moment before glancing down at his own elegant watch. 'It's almost ten.'

Gracie took the chance to leap back towards her open doorway. 'Wow! That late?'

'Don't worry about it. I insisted the staff let you enjoy as much sleep as you required.'

'Well, thanks. But now I'm up I'd better get ready. For Mila. Don't want the boss to think I'm slacking off on my first day on the job.' Damn her gibberish!

Luca spun on his heel as she scuttled through the doorway. 'I came to see if you would perhaps have lunch with me today,' Luca said, watching her impassively, leaning his elbows casually against the balustrade.

Gracie leapt inside her room and just as casually gathered a hunk of curtain, which she wound about her waist. 'Sure,' she said. 'Perhaps we can hatch a plan of action on how to find my father.'

'Sounds fine.'

'Oh, and I came down to see you last night in order to beg the use of a telephone but it slipped my mind.'

Luca sent her a brief nod, his eyes glittering in appreciation for why it might have slipped her mind. Perhaps he had not pigeonholed her after all. And perhaps that was actually a worse implication than if he had.

'The only one is in my office, but please feel free to use it any time. Consider it a perk of the job.'

Gracie shot him a thin-lipped smile.

'One o'clock in my office,' Luca said. 'I think you know the way.'

'I do. See you then.' Gracie shot him a jaunty salute before disappearing inside her room, slamming the doors and drawing the curtains as tight as they would go.

Thank God I shaved my legs, she thought as she loped the several steps to her bed, where she collapsed face down, giggling and burying her blushing face in the cool cotton sheets.

Luca stood staring at the decidedly closed door for several moments more. He blinked long and slow but it still didn't dissolve the image branded across his vision.

He'd come out of his bedroom after returning home from church, looking for a little sunshine with which to kick-start his working day, and he had been afforded a view infinitely more warming.

His daughter's new English tutor was leaning against the railing, her faded T-shirt barely covering the cheeks of her bottom, her long, smooth, delectably curved legs bare to the morning sun, with one fluffy-sock-clad foot tucking atop of the other, staving off the cool of the concrete floor. In his wildest dreams he would not have expected to find such a package under that ragged jacket and dirty denim.

He had already decided to disappear back inside his room, but Caesar's scrambling had alerted Gracie to the fact he was there so he had no choice but to bluster on over and say his good-mornings.

Her discomfort was evident as she had wrestled with her meagre clothing, doing all she could to cover herself. But she'd had no idea that her squirming only demonstrated that she wore nothing beneath her faded top.

Something inside him had stirred. Something quite

apart from the instant awareness such a sudden view would give any red-blooded man. Luca had always been with women with an obvious measure of sophistication. His Sarina would not have been seen dead in such a get-up, preferring the latest sexy, slippery designs from the top Italian lingerie designers. As such, Luca was surprised to find himself moved by Gracie's artless modesty. And he had no right to be stirred.

Luca rolled his shoulder and turned his attention away from the closed windows and towards his grounds, wondering why he had really invited this stranger, this ingenuous spitfire, into his home to help look after his precious daughter. True, he had already checked her references, which had been beyond glowing. This was a woman well-loved and much missed back home. According to her previous employers, she often sneaked into the casino crèche in her break time, teaching the kids funny songs that drove the carers insane. He had laughed aloud at that one, absolutely believing it to be true.

Suddenly there was a thud from inside Gracie's room, followed by a loudly exclaimed oath. He was pretty sure she had stubbed her toe.

It brought a smile to his face. That was why he had brought her here. His beloved home had begun to feel stale. It was so long since it had had any spark, and he knew this slip of a girl could provide it in her sleep.

He heard a continued thumping. He pictured her hopping on one leg, her curls bouncing about her ears, her odd T-shirt hiking up as she grabbed a hold of her sore toe…

Caesar licked Luca's hand. He gave the big dog a scratch behind the ear. 'I know. Down, boy, right?'

Luca shook his head and dragged himself away from

the balustrade and back to his own room with Caesar following behind. It was time to get his mind back where it belonged—on work, not on the state of undress of his daughter's new English tutor.

CHAPTER FOUR

DRESSED more appropriately in rolled-up khaki cargo pants, sandshoes and a black sleeveless top, her hair in friendly pigtails, Gracie followed Cat's directions and found Mila's bedroom, or girl heaven, as it could have been called.

Mila, trussed up in a navy velvet dress, white tights and black patent shoes, had every toy a little girl could want in her frilly pink room. Teddy bears of all shapes and sizes sat upon every available surface. The most unbelievable doll's house took up one corner and a beautiful rocking-horse had pride of place in another. She sat in the middle of the massive room, half-submerged in the lush pile carpet, with her ever-present toy horse in her hand.

'Good morning, Mila,' Gracie said from the doorway.

Mila looked up at Gracie with imperious eyes. 'I know more English than anyone in the house apart from Papa. What are you going to teach me?'

Hmm. It seemed the honeymoon was over. This gig was not going to be as easy as Luca had suggested. It would not be all long lunches and chasing pigeons with a bit of English thrown in for good measure. Gracie felt her palms sweat, but she knew she had no choice but to give it a go. Taking a deep breath, she sat down on the floor with Mila.

'If you know so much English already, what else is there you would like to know?' Gracie asked, and it was a question that wiped the commanding look from Mila's face. She was only four, for goodness' sake. People asked her what she would like to eat, what she would like to wear and where she would like to go. But Gracie had counted on the fact that nobody asked her what she would like to *know*.

She pierced Gracie with a steady glance and asked, 'I would like to know what heaven is like.'

Gracie deserved that. Baiting a four-year-old was only going to bring the gods frowning down upon her. 'What do *you* think heaven is like?' Gracie lobbed back.

Mila thought about it for a moment. 'I think it's a lot like here.'

Gracie nodded, thinking of the sumptuous house with its lush gardens. 'Sounds about right to me, Mila. Heaven is somewhere beautiful where your mum is very happy.'

'Then it's not like here,' Mila said, and her sweet face crumpled.

'Why do you say that, sweetie? Don't you think this is the most beautiful place on earth?'

Mila nodded solemnly and Gracie realised what she was getting at. She shuffled in closer on the pretence of taking a doll and brushing its hair. Her leg ended up resting casually against Mila's, and the little girl shifted until they were cocooned against one another.

'But your mum wasn't happy here,' Gracie deduced.

Mila shook her head. 'She used to dream of big cities.'

'Did she tell you that?'

Mila nodded as she brushed her plastic pony's hair with an imaginary brush. 'When she thought I was sleeping, she would pat my hair and tell me of her days and nights in big cities when she was young and beautiful.'

'Did you ever tell your *papa* this? Or Gran-nonna?'

'No. It was not important. It was just a dream.'

Gracie remembered Luca's set jaw when they had pulled up to the villa. The way his whole body had clenched when he had called his beautiful home 'isolated'. Luca knew of his wife's dream, and for the first time Gracie wondered at how perfect Luca's family had in fact been.

'Maybe heaven for her is like a city, then,' Mila wondered aloud.

Gracie had had enough of watching the poor little thing struggle. She grabbed her around the waist and shunted her onto her lap, tickling as she went. 'Whatever her heaven is like, I can guarantee she has the prime view watching over you every day.'

Mila turned to look Gracie dead in the eye for the first time since the conversation had begun.

'Otherwise it wouldn't be heaven, now, would it?' Gracie explained.

Mila blinked then gave Gracie the biggest hug she could manage before she squirmed and wiggled her way back onto the floor and ran out the door.

'Enough English,' she said over her shoulder. 'Time for Gracie to learn some *Italiano. Venuto.*'

'*Venuto?* I've already learnt that one,' Gracie said to the empty doorway. She dragged herself back to her feet and followed. 'Where are we going?' she called out as she followed the quick young girl down the elegant staircase.

Gracie shot a look to Luca's half-open doorway but she could hear no noise from within. If he had heard their scampering footsteps, perhaps he would be persuaded to come join them, to leave his dark office and *venuto* into the sunshine. But even after one final glance over her shoulder from the other end of the foyer, there was no sign of the man. Feeling oddly disappointed, Gracie had no choice but to follow Mila out the back door.

'Pino needs a drink,' Mila said, waving her toy horse in the air.

From nowhere Caesar came bounding after them, circling Mila, who was half his size. So far the dog seemed to do nothing worse than slobber, bark and jog, but instinct brought Gracie straight to Mila's side. She took a hold of Mila's hand.

'*Tallone!*' Mila commanded and the bear of a dog relaxed into a contented trot at her side. 'That means heel,' Mila said.

'Cool bananas,' Gracie said, seriously impressed.

Mila smiled up at her and led her away from the house and further into the grounds.

Gracie breathed in the fresh Tuscan air as they trekked along the beautiful lawn she had been admiring from up on high earlier. Down on the ground it was just as charming, if possible even more so. She let herself be led as she revelled in the peaceful beauty of the estate. The memory of sharing the experience with Luca whilst barely dressed added a kind of funky edge to the experience.

There was no denying it; the guy set her pulse a-racing. Day. Night. Sharing pasta or a view. It didn't seem to matter.

Gracie, who was used to fending off marriage proposals without breaking pace dealing out a deck of cards, and who could fend off a wandering hand using only the strength in her thumb, found herself distracted beyond comfort by this one quiet Italian gent. He could flirt with the best of them, and the constant glimmer in his smiling eyes spoke volumes, but he had still been nothing but polite and gentlemanly towards her.

Maybe that was the difference. He was nice to her. Nastiness she could fend off with a withering glance. Sarcasm she could hit out of the ballpark. But nice—what could one do to defend oneself against that?

A stray dove flew too low and Caesar took off after it, his deep barks resonating until he rounded the hillside and was gone.

'Is he OK?' Gracie asked, hoping she would not be called upon to chase after him.

Mila shrugged. 'Of course. He will come home when he is hungry.'

'Fair enough.'

As they skirted around the edge of the stables Gracie pointed out different areas of interest, making sure Mila could name them in English. The girl knew it all. They hit the edge of the woodland and Gracie made Mila count the number of steps aloud in English. She didn't get one number out of place.

By the time they reached the creek, Gracie had almost given up. She grabbed Mila into her arms as she skipped over several large flat stepping-stones to reach the flat grassy bank on the other side.

'Jeepers creepers,' she whispered against Mila's ear, 'you are just too clever for your own good.'

When she set Mila down, the little girl turned her way with a glint in her eye. 'Cheepers? What are cheepers?'

Gracie shot out an accusing finger. 'Ha! I can teach you something.'

Gracie set about teaching Mila an assortment of extremely important lingo that the young girl assured her she could no longer live without. After half an hour of solid work, Mila had had enough. Gracie lay on the grassy bank watching her as she led her toy horse to water.

She was a gorgeous girl. Polite. Clever. Cute as a button. But a tad serious. Gracie was sure she got that from her father. They both had the same crinkle above their noses as though they were constantly in deep thought.

Simply being in these beautiful surroundings, spending time with these good people, it would be all too easy to forget why she was really there, to happily forget and pretend that this was where she belonged, in some fairy-tale castle with the almost perfect family, who needed her in that moment as much as she needed them.

But her real family was out there somewhere. Her father was close. She had to find him. Until that part of her past was sorted, her future was a blur.

She lay on her back and watched the fluffy white clouds float past the treetops and wondered for about the millionth time if any of her personality traits had come from her father. Was he the life of the party? Was he allergic to early mornings and exercise? Was he a genius at working public transport systems? She was certain she had assumed none of those traits from her conservative, up-with-the-birds, tennis-playing, car-pooling mother.

Gracie was brought back to the present as a great fluffy lump sat upon her legs. She was not quick enough to stop an effusive 'Hell's bells!' from escaping her lips.

Thinking it some sort of endearment, the newly arrived Caesar shifted his weight so that he could pin Gracie to the ground and lick her about the face. Gracie half expected to die of fright but instead found the ticklish experience hilarious. She grabbed the dog about the scruff of the neck and roughed him up as she had seen Luca do. He rolled over onto his back and took the abuse with noisy snuffles and a lolling tongue.

Feeling pretty proud of herself for facing down the bear, for teaching Mila some new words, for being pretty darned good at this gig after all, Gracie stood to her feet and brushed herself down. 'Come on, Mila, sweetie. Time we headed back.'

Suddenly Mila let out a great screeching wail. All thoughts of her own family problems and her misguided pride were obliterated in a flash as her mind slammed with the image of Mila injured. Gracie was at her side in an instant. She slid to her knees in the soft grass and took Mila by the shoulders. 'What is it, sweetie?'

Mila was weeping in huge racking sobs. Gracie swallowed down her panic. What had she been thinking, daydreaming by a creek with a four-year-old at her side? What had she been thinking in taking on this job? She knew nothing about kids. Had Mila been stung by something? Had she wet her pants? Gracie didn't even know where to begin.

Thankfully, Mila was not one to keep secrets. 'It's Pino!'

'Pino?' Gracie racked her brain for the English translation. Then it occurred to her. 'Oh, your horse!'

Mila pointed to the creek, where plastic Pino was floating sideways, drifting happily out into the centre of the waterway. 'He was drinking and he fell in.'

'OK, sweetie. Don't panic. You stay here and I'll go and get him.' Gracie made sure Mila understood before letting her go.

Mila nodded, her nose crinkle deepening by the second.

Gracie walked out onto the stepping-stones. Pino was within reach. Or maybe not. She crouched and stretched but Pino bobbed just out of reach. Mila's sniffles deepened and became more panicked. With one look at the forlorn little girl, Gracie whispered under her breath, 'Stuff it,' before stepping into the thigh-high depths.

The icy cold hit her straight away. 'Jeepers creepers,'

she said, her voice warbling with an instant shiver. But Mila's sniffly giggle was enough to keep her going.

She trod carefully over the slippery stones that lay along the creek floor. She grabbed Pino and held him above head height, making sure Mila knew he was just fine. But a few steps on, her sandshoe slipped, and she slid straight beneath the water. The water, which was basically a product of melting snow from nearby mountains, was that bitter it sapped her breath clean away.

Only a moment later she broke the surface, raking in a great, gaping breath, and bit back the language she ached to let forth, knowing Mila was a quick leaner. Not as though she would have heard a thing over Caesar's echoing barks.

The biting cold and her fear for Mila's sensitive nerves had her out of that water quicker than she imagined she could be. Back on the shore, breathing heavily, feeling like a drowned rat, Gracie looked up to find Mila giggling so hard her curls jiggled about her face.

'Are you laughing at me, Miss Siracusa?'

Mila bit her lip and shook her head.

'Perhaps Pino has had enough of an adventure for one day. Time we return to the house?' Gracie suggested.

Mila took her by the hand and didn't once try to pull ahead. The midday sun was out in full strength so they took the long way, around the wood and to the front of the property, down through the line of conical trees. As soon as she had dried off, she would get Mila inside for a quick nap. Before lunch with Luca, she wanted to let the embassy know where she could be reached in case they had any information. She chastised herself mentally for already wasting half a day without doing so. Maybe they had already tried her at the hostel but she had not left a forwarding number with Enzo.

Gracie trudged wetly while Mila flitted and Caesar bounded. Surely Mila would soon wind down. Gracie herself was fast losing pace. Where the young girl found her energy, Gracie had no idea. It said something for a diet of pasta and fresh garden salads versus a diet of take-away pizza and sweets.

Suddenly Caesar barked and took off for the house, and Mila yanked on Gracie's arm so hard she let go, allowing Mila to sprint off in the same direction, shouting something unintelligible to Gracie's neophyte ears. After stopping to indulge in an unfit groan, Gracie lengthened her stride so Mila did not get too far ahead.

Only then did she spot the unfamiliar car in the driveway. It was metallic blue, sporty and convertible.

Gracie ran a hand over her damp clumped pigtails and pulled her wet black top away from her body, flapping it to try to dry it quicker. Since Mila had already made a noisy run up the front steps she knew there was no point in taking the side-entrance into the house. She had to follow her charge. In any case, whoever the visitor was, they were not there to see her.

At the top of the steps, Gracie took off her squelching sandshoes and tied the laces together then hung the shoes over her right shoulder. Barefoot and dripping with creek water, Gracie entered the house ready to meet the newcomer before making a polite exit to maintain her date with the telephone.

'Zia Jemma!' Mila cried, flying into the arms of a svelte young woman who looked as if she had stepped out of the pages of *You're Too Skinny, Eat!* magazine. Even so, she caught Mila on the fly and swung her up onto her slim hip. She passed a present to Mila, who eyed it and shook it.

'Come siete?' Jemma asked in Italian.

'Fabulous,' Mila said in English.

The young woman's thin eyebrows shot skyward. 'Fabulous?' she repeated in a thick accent.

Mila giggled into her shoulder.

'Mila is having English lessons,' Luca said from somewhere behind Gracie.

She spun around to find him striding towards her, a surprised smile lighting his face, Caesar trotting merrily at his master's side. He raised an eyebrow in her direction and Gracie stared right back, this time managing to stop herself from poking out her tongue.

As Luca strode past, Gracie caught a whiff of his aftershave. The scent was drinkable.

She continued her spin to find the lovely Jemma watching her carefully.

'Gracie,' he said loud enough for the others to hear, 'this is Jemma Malfi, my sister-in-law and Mila's aunt. Jemma, this is Gracie Lane, Mila's English tutor.'

Luca reached Jemma and placed a kiss on each cheek, but Jemma's eyes never left Gracie's face.

'Why does Mila need an English teacher?' Jemma asked Luca whilst still staring Gracie down. 'I can teach her well if that is what you like?'

'Thank you, Jemma. But I am quite happy with this arrangement.' For the first time in their short acquaintance, Gracie heard Luca's chairman-of-the-board voice. It was soft yet insistent. Nice, but with more than a hint of steel beneath it. She liked it.

Jemma was obviously not impressed. Gracie felt like the third wheel in some sort of lovers' tiff. But not quite. Jemma was watching her carefully, but not jealously. It was a different sort of dynamic, of that she was sure.

'What has she learnt from this woman that she could not have learnt from any of us?'

Mila finally tore open her present and, seeing a tiny saddle that would fit Pino perfectly, she squealed, 'Cool bananas!'

A great loud laugh escaped from Gracie's mouth. She slapped a hand over her lips and bit down hard. Luca ducked his head to hide his own matching grin.

'It seems Mila has answered the question for me,' Jemma said with wide eyes. 'I wouldn't even begin to know what that might mean. Maybe you could teach us all a thing or two, Miss Lane.' Jemma gave her a warm smile that spoke of a fast thaw. Huh. Well, there you go.

A bell rang throughout the house.

'Ah,' Luca said, 'it seems lunch is ready. Jemma, you will join us, I hope.'

'*Sì,*' Jemma said, returning her attention to her niece in an instant.

'*Buono.*'

Gracie had no idea if she was invited to the family lunch so she made to retire as gracefully as she could. She clapped her hands together to grab everyone's attention. 'Right, then, I hope you don't mind if leave you to it. I need to run up and change.'

'Then you will return and join us, I hope,' Luca said, doing his mind-reading trick again.

'Thank you, I will.'

Luca shot Gracie a look full of apology. It seemed their private chat would have to wait. Gracie sent back an eloquent shrug before taking the stairs two at a time with the joy of a hot shower at the end of it.

The vision that met her in the mirror was worse than she had imagined. The shoulders of her top were twisted, revealing the hot-pink bra straps beneath. Her cargo pants were suctioned to her legs, showcasing every curve and the fact she wore a pretty teeny G-string beneath. Her

pigtails were wet, clumped and curling. Her cheeks were
pink from the unaccustomed sunshine. All in all she
looked like a street urchin who had been playing in a burst
water main.

'Good one, Gracie. Way to make an impression. But
who are you trying to make an impression on?' she asked
her reflection. Then, pointing at herself, she demanded,
'Nobody, that's who.'

With a self-chastising growl Gracie whipped the clothes
from her body, stood under a short hot shower, then raked
her hair back into a towel-dried pony-tail. She changed
into clean jeans and the only other T-shirt Cat had left
when she had taken her washing, the one with an Aussie
flag splayed across the chest with a smiley face in the
place of the Union Jack. It had been a going-away present
from Kelly and Cara along with a packet of emergency
chocolate Tim-Tams—which she had eaten on the flight
over—and a pre-paid phone card—which she had barely
used to call home.

After lunch, she promised herself, pulling the phone
card from her passport pack and laying it on the dresser.
I'll call the embassy after lunch. Home could wait.

Feeling underdressed compared with the glamorous
Jemma, but at least less like a contestant in a wet-T-shirt
competition, she headed downstairs to the dining room.
Luca sat at the head of the table with Mila to his right
and Jemma to his left. Gracie had no choice but to take
the only remaining seat at the other end of the table.

'Gracie, Mila has been too busy playing with Pino's
new saddle to fill us in on your little adventure. Perhaps
you would be so kind.'

'I went for a swim,' she said, with as straight a face as
she could muster. 'No biggie—'

'You did not,' Mila interrupted. 'You saved Pino's life!'

'Fine,' Gracie said with a dramatic roll of her eyes. 'It all started because Pino wanted to have a drink…'

Luca leant back in his chair and watched the animated conversation progress.

Jemma, so like her sister, fussed over Mila, wiping away crumbs with her napkin, telling her to sit up straight, making sure she acted like a little lady.

Mila had never reacted well under such duress, even as a baby. She continuously wriggled out of Jemma's way until her aunt gave up, throwing her napkin to the table in dramatic abandon.

Gracie, on the other hand, didn't pander to Mila's stubbornness for a second. Nobody else would have known that she was paying any attention to what Mila was up to during her lively and hilarious narrative. But when Mila's obstinacy towards Jemma threatened to reach an awkward crescendo, Gracie called out, 'Mila!'

Everyone at the table jumped with her sudden change of subject. But then she softened the remonstration with, 'Don't you want my *gelato*? I only ate the lemon.'

Luca watched Mila's mouth fly open to complain, but then the wheels in her mind turned and she realised it was in her best interest to play the good girl.

'Yes, please,' Mila said, and hummed happily as she ate the second helping of dessert.

Gracie continued her story as though nothing had happened but Luca saw that her eyes kept flicking back to make sure Mila continued behaving.

He leant his head on his palm. It was a warm afternoon, but there was something else making him feel relaxed, making him feel as though the day was going by in contented slow motion.

It was Gracie, stranger and stray.

He couldn't believe that he had been so taken with the woman he had not even been able to let her out of his sight after a five-minute conversation. Her bright blue eyes in her fair face sparkled with the palpable vitality that had compelled him to offer the bargain in the first place. Her delight warmed him. Thawing him. Stimulating the shield that had settled around his heart for so long, he thought it would never go away.

With the thaw came discomfort. But something was willing him to follow through on his reinvigorated instincts. The very same instincts he had vowed never to trust again.

CHAPTER FIVE

HALF an hour later Luca stood at the front door, one arm draped around Jemma's slim shoulders as he watched Gracie play with his daughter.

She had Mila on her hip and was swinging her around and around out on the gravel driveway and Mila was hanging on for dear life, squealing with a mix of fear and pleasure. He knew his daughter was irrepressible and that she had a short attention span, but somehow Gracie managed to keep her amused. He'd never seen anyone with that sort of patience or success with his clever daughter. Never.

'She is a sweet girl,' Jemma said, reverting to their native tongue.

He smiled down at her and she tucked herself into his side. 'Of course she is,' he said. 'Just like her mother. And her aunt.'

Jemma looked into his eyes. 'I did not mean Mila, Luca, and you know it.'

Luca watched in silence as Gracie dropped Mila to the ground, encouraging her to stand atop her feet as she taught the younger girl to dance. Mila's eyes were glued to her feet, her attention appropriated all too easily by the vivacious woman at her side.

'I hope you know what you are doing,' Jemma said.

He gave her a companionable squeeze. 'I'm afraid I have no idea what you mean.'

'Fine,' Jemma said, 'then I will not beat around the

bush. Be careful, brother. I do not think you want Mila to get attached to another woman who will soon leave her.'

Luca licked his suddenly dry lips. Of course that concern had needled at him, but he had managed to think his way around it. 'We have an arrangement. Gracie is only in Italy for a finite amount of time. She will teach Mila some international English whilst she is here, but she has never expressed any wish to stay long enough for Mila to garner any real attachment. It is a perfect arrangement.'

'Hmm. We'll see. What does Miss Lane get from this whole experience? A notation on her résumé?'

Luca knew he couldn't fill Jemma in on the circumstances of his deal with Gracie. It would be breaking a confidence. But he could twist the truth in order to reiterate that this was definitely short-term.

'Miss Lane is on holiday. She is happy to teach Mila so that she can see some of the countryside. Then she will move on.'

'And Mila?'

'Mila will be fine. She has me, and Gran-nonna, and you.'

'And yet already she clings to this one like a limpet.'

As though sensing they were talking about her, Gracie squinted up at them, her dark blue eyes unreadable at that distance.

'I've said my piece,' Jemma said. She gave Luca a kiss on each cheek before stepping lightly down the steps and across to the other two girls.

Mila kept a tight hold of Gracie and leant back for her kiss from Jemma, trusting all the while that Gracie would not let her fall.

'You are leaving?' Gracie asked Jemma. She dropped a squirming Mila to the ground and watched distractedly as the little girl skipped over to her father, who watched her with such concentration her heart rate doubled.

'I must,' Jemma said. 'I really only came for a quick visit to drop off some jam to the kitchen staff. My mother makes it from the fruits of our orchard.'

'Why didn't your mother drop it off?' Gracie asked, dragging her gaze back from watching Luca and Mila to find a remote look in Jemma's eyes.

Jemma pulled a face as she waved away the notion with a flapping of her hands. 'They are old. They are stubborn—'

'And they blame Luca somehow for your sister's death.'

Jemma's mouth hung open for a brief moment before she nodded. 'That they do.'

Wow. For Luca the hits just kept on coming. Gracie felt an odd welling of protection rush through her veins. 'But how could they? How did it happen?'

'Single-car crash. She was alone and driving too fast. Her car spun out of control and hit a tree.' Jemma shrugged. 'I don't think there is any definitive reason why they blame dear Luca, except that she is gone and he couldn't save her.'

Save her? Gracie wondered. *From what?* Mila's retelling of her mother's wishes to live a bright life in the city began to take on new resonance.

'And that is enough for them not to come and see their granddaughter?' Gracie asked.

'Apparently so.'

'And Luca's parents?' So caught up in her own familial mess, Gracie had not thought to ask.

'They are long gone. They passed away within weeks of one another during the years when Luca was away at school. It was when he returned home for his father's funeral that he and Sarina decided to marry.'

'*Decided* to marry?' Gracie repeated.

'But Mila is not wanting for company,' Jemma continued unabated. 'I pop in twice a week at least and Luca is always around. There are plenty of musty old adults about to drive Mila crazy. And now she has you too.'

Gracie felt an odd shift in the conversation and knew that Jemma's words weren't all as light and fluffy as she would have had Gracie believe. 'For a good time, not a long time,' she insisted with a big smile.

'If you say so.' Jemma moved towards her flashy car, and suddenly Gracie felt anxious about her leaving. She looked up to the front door to find the space now empty. Luca and Mila must have retired indoors.

'I thought you might stay a while longer,' Gracie said. 'I'm sure Mila would love to have you stay. And Luca as well.'

'Luca puts up with my constant uninvited comings and goings, but I will not impose more than I already have. I assure you Luca will be glad of it.' Jemma's smile was brimming with understanding and Gracie wished it wasn't. 'You will all be fine here without me.'

Boy, how Gracie wished this young woman were staying. It only made her realise how much she missed Kelly and Cara. How much she wanted to talk about…stuff. Including the odd desire not to be left alone with her host.

'OK,' Gracie said. 'I hope to see you again soon.'

'I hope so too,' Jemma said with a grin. She planted a kiss on both of Gracie's cheeks, slid behind the wheel of her glamorous car, then in a swirl of gravel and spinning tyres her newfound ally was gone.

Gracie meandered slowly back into the house to find Mila had taken up residence in Luca's office. Luca was resting against his desk, his arms folded across his broad chest and his legs crossed at the ankles. He was watching his daughter with that same quiet rapture with which he always looked upon her. He looked up as she knocked.

'Hi,' he said with a smile straight out of a cologne commercial.

'Hi,' she said, her voice croaky.

'Would you like to have that chat now?' he asked, his voice deep and rich and resonant. It sent a shiver down Gracie's back.

She would have loved nothing more than to get down to planning on how to find her dad, but she had to get out of there. All that manliness amongst all that dark wood and leather furniture was just too overwhelming. She was getting ideas and ideas were the last thing she needed to be having about her great white hope.

'Um, not now. I was thinking of taking Mila to visit Gran-nonna,' Gracie said, pleased with her quick thinking.

Luca nodded. 'OK. Mila?' he called, his eyes taking their sweet time to leave Gracie and turn to his daughter, who was back on the sheepskin rug by his desk.

'*Sì?*'

'Gracie is going to take you to visit Gran-nonna.'

'No.'

The mood in the room changed in an instant as three wills collided.

'No?' Luca repeated, peeling himself away from the desk.

Mila stopped playing for a second as she sensed her father's displeasure, but she set her teeth and shook her head so hard her curls whipped her face. 'No!'

Gracie didn't know whether she should stay or go, if she should interfere or leave it up to Luca. But then she felt his indecision. He was obviously unhappy with Mila's stubbornness but didn't have it in him to make her do something she did not want to do.

The girl was too spoilt. Luca had admitted as much himself. With a great sigh, Gracie leapt into the fray.

'Come on, Mila. Your dad has lots of work to do so we are going to visit your *gran-nonna*. Now.'

Mila's bottom lip trembled. 'She lives on our property and only comes to dinner once a week. Why should we have to visit her?'

Hmm. Time to pull out the big guns.

'Don't you think it would be lonely if *you* had to live at the other end of the property and only saw your dad once in a while?'

Mila's eyes widened and her horrified gaze flickered from Gracie to her father, who took up the slack and nodded with gusto.

Gracie continued, 'How about we take some of Jemma's jam and go over to Gran-nonna's and have a tea party?'

The mix of guilt, fear and the promise of a tea party did the trick. 'Is Pino invited?' Mila asked.

'Of course,' Gracie said. 'You must always have an even number at a tea party so everybody has somebody to look at across the table.' She held out her hand. 'Coming?'

Mila looked to Pino and found all the support she needed. She stood and took Gracie by the hand.

Gracie flicked a last glance in Luca's direction before they left. 'We won't be long. I'll have her home for a nap before dinner.'

Luca nodded. 'Sure. Thanks.' His face was lit with wonder at how she had managed to turn a situation fraught with the probability of tears into such a positive outcome. The poor guy had no idea how to keep his daughter in line. Or more likely he had no real desire to do so. It was terribly sweet. And terribly overdue for a fix.

'No worries,' she assured him, determined not to focus on that sweetness for too long.

'See you later, then.'

'Bye.' Gracie dragged Mila out of the office before the two of them became caught in a loop of inanities, just so she could get an eternal kick out of looking into Luca's trusting, astonished and admiring face.

A girl could have her head turned permanently if she wasn't extra-careful.

Later that day, after a truly memorable afternoon spent with a little girl, her great-grandmother and a toy horse, Gracie settled Mila down for an afternoon nap. After the events of the day she could have happily joined her, but she had to take advantage of her down time for more pressing matters.

Her bare feet shuffling quietly, her hand stifling a yawn, Gracie approached Luca's office door. All was quiet. She knocked. Nothing. She pushed open the door. Still nothing. Luca's laptop was on but sleeping, his desk light was turned off, and there was no sign of Caesar. But next to his laptop sat a telephone.

Luca had assured her the phone was hers to use as she pleased. And it pleased her to use it to call the Australian Embassy.

She walked slowly to the desk, her heart racing, and sat in Luca's cool leather chair. She picked up the cordless phone, typed in the phone number and waited as the ringing line sounded ominously in her ear.

Blood pounded in her ears as she waited for the chirpy voice to come on to the line and…what? Tell her they had found him and he was waiting to hear from her?

Tell her they had found him and he wanted nothing to do with her? Tell her they had found him, but he was no longer—?

'Miss Lane!' The woman's voice with its heartening Australian accent shot through the earpiece. 'We have been trying to contact you!'

Oh, God! They've found him! They have found him and they have been trying to tell me, but I've been keeping him waiting.

Gracie let out a choked, 'Sorry. I have moved. Have you…have you found him?'

'Sorry, darling. Nothing. *Nada.* But…the good news is we are having an ex-pat party here next month and were wondering if you would like to be added to the guest list.'

Gracie blinked as she tried to compute what the woman was telling her. 'A party?'

'Yep. For Australians living in Rome. Coming?'

Gracie's disappointment was mingled with a strange sort of joy that at least there was still hope for it all turning out OK. 'Is it OK if l get back to you?' she managed to ask.

'Sure. No rush.'

Gracie fumbled her way through the rest of the conversation, leaving her new forwarding address and phone number. She slid the phone back into its cradle and stared at it through wide, unblinking eyes. Her body rocked with a violent shiver. She thanked her lucky stars, or Neptune, or whoever had made it possible for her to come to Luca's home. If she hadn't she would have been home by now.

Images flashed through her mind. Images of Kelly and Cara seeing her off at the airport all those weeks ago, hugs filled with optimism and good wishes. Images of her quiet half-sister and half-brother sitting still and polite on the family couch as Gracie slipped out of her mother's wake early.

The little red indicator light on the phone glared back at her accusingly. Call home, it insisted. Tell them you are sorry. Tell them you are scared. Tell them you are missing them. Tell them you are in one piece, sort of.

But she couldn't. Didn't want to. Not yet. Not until she had some happy news. They were all people who deserved nothing bar happy news.

But did *she*? Was that the problem? Was this heart-wrenching quest all some sort of punishment for not being more understanding to her mother when it was just the two of them? For not being more accommodating when there were suddenly five of them? And for not knowing how to feel, how to cope, how to grieve, when one of them was gone?

Footsteps on the polished wood floor of the foyer roused Gracie from her reverie. Luca opened the door and only noticed her once he was halfway inside the office.

'Sorry,' he said, taking a step backwards. 'Am I disturbing you?'

'Not at all,' she said, her voice unnaturally husky. 'Mila is taking a nap, so I just called… I was using the phone.'

His eyes narrowed and Gracie knew he could tell she was distracted.

'It was the Australian Embassy,' she admitted. 'No news is good news, right?' She tried a self-deprecating smile on for size but knew by Luca's frown that it didn't fit.

'I can come back later,' he suggested, motioning to the open doorway, 'if you need more time.'

Gracie stood and ran her shaking hands down her sides, wiping away the moisture. 'No, please. I'm done. I'll leave you to get back to work.'

He moved further into the office, blocking her escape. 'Actually, I was about to call the kitchen for *biscotti* and espresso. Would you care to join me?'

Gracie scuffed a bare foot against the hardwood floor. The thought of being left alone with her thoughts did not appeal right at that moment. Biscuits, coffee and polite conversation did. She felt as if she was little more than a big, beating, open wound, so she moved carefully while the floundering pieces of herself struggled back together. 'Sure, why not?'

Luca held out an arm towards the inviting leather couch Mila had fallen asleep upon the night before. Gracie took a seat. Caesar appeared from nowhere as usual and sat on her feet. He looked up at her with such easy amity, and it made her feel a very little bit better. She scratched behind his ear in thanks.

After ordering their afternoon coffee, Luca joined Gracie on the couch. 'How are you finding your time here so far?'

'It's beautiful. Truly. I can't believe I've been here only twenty-four hours. It already feels like—'

'Home?' he asked, with an undemanding smile.

Gracie gave him an indefinite shrug. 'I guess I have been on the go for so long it's nice to stop and put my feet up for a little while. I wanted to thank you for going out of your way to help a woman on the edge.'

A small smile played about Luca's lips. 'You do have a way with words, *bella*.'

'That's what I am here for.'

'Mmm. And, as such, you are helping me also. I have achieved more work today than I have in a long time. I had forgotten what it feels like to start a thought and be able to finish it. *Grazie*.'

'My pleasure.'

Luca's responding smile lit up the room. It kicked at something deep inside her stomach. Something that didn't need to be kicked. It had to remain decidedly unkicked. She was susceptible. She knew that. In making the decision to find her father, she had opened her heart to the chance of success, of failure, of happiness, of disappointment, and it had made her vulnerable to other feelings as well.

'Does Mila always sit in with you whilst you work?' Gracie asked, shifting to tuck a foot beneath her, and to put some space between her and the object of her concerns.

'Pretty much,' he said after a thoughtful moment.

'Did you have to stop yourself from coming to see her today?'

Luca's eyes zeroed in on hers as he did that total, breathtaking focus thing he was so good at. Gracie tried, unsuccessfully, not to let the sensation rocket through her body.

'Many times,' he admitted.

'So what stopped you?' She knew she was putting out a challenge to him to join them in the future.

'I don't rightly know,' he said, slowly, deliberately, and she knew she now had him seriously thinking about it.

She was the one who needed the kick, not her stomach. Maybe it was the warm room, maybe it was the low lighting, maybe it was the silence apart from the quiet whirr of the computer motor near by. Whatever it was, Gracie was succumbing to the complete joy of being with the man. But there was nothing to be gained from it.

He was newly widowed.

She was basically under his employ.

He was going to help her find her father.

And unless she found a way to control her skittishness around him, the whole delicately stacked house of cards could come tumbling down around her bare feet.

Cat came in with a tray laden with biscuits and espressos. Never one to let a good sweet pass her by, Gracie grabbed a selection.

Luca was first off the mark as soon as they were alone again. 'Tell me a little bit about your life back in Australia. Do you have sisters and brothers?'

The warmth of the room slipped away and Gracie felt a chill overcome her as the wound opened up again. 'One of each. Both a good deal younger. And both half-siblings, obviously.'

'Mmm. You are so good with Mila, I knew you must have had more experience than you let on.'

Gracie shook her head then lowered it. 'Not really. I left home when they were only little and haven't actually had that much to do with them since.'

Gracie pictured the last time she had spent any real time with them. The two lanky blondes, red-faced and shocked, standing looking over their mother's grave. Being older, Gracie had the luxury of being able to put some very real distance, physical and emotional, between herself and that difficult moment. They did not. She felt a deep pang of regret that she had not spent more time helping them deal with their loss, which must have been as great if not greater than her own.

'I am surprised. Yet not,' Luca said, crowding into her muddied thoughts. 'I think you are what they call a people person.'

Not recently, she thought. But all she said was, 'I have my moments.' Gracie bit down on the most melt-in-your-mouth biscuit she had ever eaten, and she was a girl who knew her biscuits.

'Tell me more about Australia,' Luca urged. 'I have travelled some, but never that far. Never far enough to need to be in the air for twenty-four hours to get there.'

'Well, it's true that we each own a kangaroo as a pet, and that all Australians are blonde and can surf before they can walk.'

Luca's smile was indulgent. 'Even if I were not privy to the fact that you enjoy trapping the locals with your wily English, I would know that you are pulling my leg. You have not a lick of blonde in this raven hair of yours.'

He reached out and wrapped a stray curl around his finger. She felt him tug lightly before letting it slip from his grasp. Then he kept talking as though nothing had happened.

'But I am not looking for the tourist guide to Australia,' he said. 'I am looking for information about the life that awaits you back home. Tell me about your friends. I believe who we choose as friends tells us a great deal about ourselves.'

Back home, Gracie thought and her chest constricted.

'My two best buds are Kelly and Cara. They live…lived in my building. We had this great deal going on the last couple of years called Saturday Night Cocktails. It was a date. A regular gig. No matter what else was going down in our lives, we knew that we always had that to look forward to.'

'Always *had*?' he asked. As always, he was too sharp.

'Within months of one another they moved out of St Kilda Storeys, our fab little apartment building by the beach. Kelly lives with her hubby, Simon, and her new baby, while Cara has been living with her boyfriend, Adam, for ages now. They still see me as much as they can but it's…different. With nobody at home to leave the light on, the time seemed just right to make this trip.'

'I see. And does their connubial bliss appeal?'

Gracie shrugged. 'For them it is perfect. But they were lucky. And I don't see lightning striking three times. It's against the odds.'

'Are you not a betting woman?'

Gracie looked up. He was watching her carefully. His dark eyes glittered in the low lamplight. He was playing with her; doing his dandiest to pull her from the doldrums.

She couldn't help but smile. 'In my profession I've seen fortunes won and lost in the blink of an eye. I don't bet.'

'Not ever?'

She thought about it for a second. Running off to a foreign country with nothing but a name to guide her was hardly a sure thing. Her smile grew despite itself. 'Never say never, right?'

The smile he sent her was slow-burning. Gracie shuffled to rouse the languor settling in her limbs. Once her foot was pinched awkwardly beneath her bottom, she felt better. More alert.

'I worked in a casino for long enough to know the house always wins. The long shot or the sure thing, it's all the same. Eventually you will lose your shirt.'

Luca's gaze swept from her face to her shirt. Gracie remembered that, though dressed conservatively now, she had been parading before him in cling-wrap pretending to be a top earlier in the day.

The smile left his face, slowly, slowly, and Gracie watched mesmerised as his tanned throat swallowed and his dark eyes grew even darker. Her breath escaped on a longing, telling sigh.

What was she doing? Sighing? Smiling? Acting so agreeable? She bit her lip.

She was alone. Lonely. Dispirited. And he had offered her assistance and a warm bed. Though that explained her fondness for the guy, it was no excuse for the stomach kicks.

Then she was hit by a light-bulb moment. Her feelings were simply products of the Italian thing.

She had dreamt of chatting up *The Godfather*'s Michael Corleone since she was a kid and the fact that she had a live Italian hunk sitting across from her was just the stuff of her teenaged fantasies coming back to haunt her. It was foolish to fall for it.

But falling for him she was. Luca's eyes raked back up to hers and saw the slow dawning of understanding pool in their warm, questioning depths. He was a smart guy. A man with hot Latin blood flowing through his veins. Soon enough he would figure out the answer.

Gracie swallowed down the warmth licking at her throat. She had to put it in perspective. She had to differentiate between Luca her last hope, and Luca the man. It would only end badly if she did not. She mentally slapped herself and, with the coolest, least flirtatious voice she could muster, changed the subject.

'Luca, I've been here almost a day and though I know you are busy, and I know you've had guests, and I have taught Mila some pretty obscure English, yet we haven't spoken about my father…'

Well, that did it. It might have been unfair to bring up Mila at that moment but it worked. Luca looked as though she had thrown a bucket of icy creek water over him. He blinked several times and looked away.

'Anyway,' she continued, seeing the fissure grow in Luca's discernment of her feelings, and leaping into it, 'I was hoping to throw some ideas at you, let you know where I've tried so far. But bear with me, as I'm not very good at thinking on my feet. It's like rubbing your stomach and patting your head at the same time.'

And Luca just stared. Gracie knew she had been blab-
bering. Now, *that* was an Aussie thing, talking way too
fast when nervous. And he made her nervous. She feared
she would have to say her speech all over again and
slower.

'Did you get any of that?' she asked.

He half nodded and half shook his head. 'You lost me
halfway, I'm afraid.'

Then his phone rang. The soft, insistent bell drew
Luca's gaze. When he looked back, his face was etched
with disappointment. 'I am sorry, Gracie. I have been
waiting for this call—'

Gracie leapt from the chair. 'No. Go ahead. We can
talk about this later. Tonight, after dinner, perhaps.' *With
the shroud of cool darkness whispering sweet nothings to
each of us.* 'Or maybe tomorrow would be better,' she
said quickly. 'Yes, tomorrow would be much better.'

Luca sent her a short nod and she had to exit gracefully.
But of course her foot had gone to sleep from her sitting
on it all that time. She tried to put pressure on it and the
pins and needles brought about an ache so sharp she all
but shouted out.

Luca took a step towards her, his arm reaching out to
guide her. The promise of his touch sent Gracie flinching
away. 'Your phone! It might be important.'

Once he was distracted, she bolted from the room,
limping and sucking in short, sharp breaths the whole way
back upstairs.

By the time she reached Mila's room, her foot was back
to normal. She gave it one last frustrated shake before
opening the door. Mila lay atop her big pink bed, asleep,
her thumb resting just inside her rosebud mouth.

The effort of keeping herself from fawning over Luca had finally sapped the last of Gracie's energy. She crept around to the far side of the bed, lay down next to the sleeping angel and was asleep within a minute.

CHAPTER SIX

AFTER Luca had finished with his phone call, his restlessness got the better of him. Gracie had basically dared him to join the two girls if he found the time. The idea of being with her…with them, appealed so much he decided to simply make the time.

He called his secretary in Rome and told her to hold all his calls for the remainder of the day. His working hours had been so varied and odd for such a long time this would not have come as a surprise.

Luca rolled his shoulders as he trudged up the long staircase. He would try Mila's room first.

The upstairs of the house was quiet. Late-afternoon sunshine streamed through the windows on the front side of the house. He loved this time of day. To him it had always seemed golden. As if the warm sunlight lit up the secret treasures the house had to offer. But it seemed one had to believe it to see it. Sarina had always laughed off his suggestion as being overly romantic and in the next breath had begged to be allowed to redesign the interior of yet another room in their already perfect home.

Mila's door was open. He poked his head in, and found a scene that astounded him.

Mila was lying on her side, snuggled up into a little ball, as she was wont to do. But, rather than looking tiny and alone as she always seemed to in her large, ruffled bed, she was engulfed in the protective form of a sleeping Gracie.

He had never once, in all the years they had been a

family, seen Sarina sleep with Mila. Love her, yes. Play with her, yes. Dress her up in the most elegant dresses their money could buy, yes. But wrap her up so tight not even the slightest breath of air could come between them, never. He had oft times wondered whether Sarina had not been as close with Mila as she could have been, but what had he known? More than he thought, apparently, because this virtual stranger found it within herself to do so within a day of meeting his gorgeous little girl.

Luca stepped quietly into the room. He was drawn to the scene as if a magnet had him in its pull.

Mila was turned away, Gracie was facing him. She had one arm draped protectively around his daughter, her palm curled in on itself, and her chest rose and fell with each languorous breath. Her dark curls, let loose from their constraining pony-tail, lay sprawled across the pillow, rippling like folds of silk. Her pale cheeks were pink from the dry warmth in the heated room. She was sleeping so soundly, all her usual sparkle and vivacity was hidden beneath her baby-smooth skin.

He sat down on the edge of the bed, the mattress sinking under his weight. He reached out and ran a hand over Gracie's warm forehead, smoothing back a stray curl that obscured her face. Her hair slipped across his fingers, sleek and soft. The movement, which had been borne of merely desiring an unencumbered view of her peaceful face, created an unanticipated ruckus in him. Her pure, soft femininity hooked deep within his chest and wouldn't let go. He swallowed, hard, but the pulsing twinge would not abate.

And then suddenly Gracie opened her eyes.

Luca sat still as a statue.

She blinked and a sleepy grin warmed her lovely face. 'Hi,' she said, her voice wafting to him on a sigh.

'Hi,' he replied, amazed he had been able to find *his* voice at all.

Then her eyes drifted closed and she was fast asleep once more.

Not willing to push his luck, Luca disentangled his fingers from her lustrous locks, turned on his heel and left. There would be no joining them today, that was for sure. But there was also no way he was going to get any work done.

As Luca strode through the house, he found evidence of Gracie everywhere. A pair of shoes, laces tied together, caked in mud, were drying by the front door. Vases filled with freshly cut wild flowers littered every table in the sitting room. Several of Mila's toys and a couple of English reading books resided under the glass coffee-table, at the ready to be used by the lady of the house.

In less than a day, the household had blossomed under her effortless warmth and enthusiasm. Just by being herself, this stranger had been able to, at long last, make his house feel like a home.

His head heavy with conflicting, dangerous, tumultuous thoughts, he stormed through the foyer and out the back door and walked the grounds at a punishing pace until the moon shed more light than the sun.

Gracie woke as Mila shuffled off the bed. She stretched like a cat in the sun after having the most delicious dream. Something had shifted as though some realisation had been made in her sleep. But it was just out of her reach. And the more awake she became the further away drifted the gossamer strands of her memory.

She sat up, her eyes adjusting to the darkness. It felt like early evening, but back home she would have had the sounds of crickets chirping and birds following the path of the dying light to settle it for her.

The noise of water came from the direction of Mila's *en suite* and a few moments later Mila padded back out to the bed.

'Sono affomato,' Mila said, rubbing her hungry tummy, her sleepiness making her kick back into her natural Italian.

'I am not surprised. It seems we slept the afternoon away. Shall we see where everyone else is?'

Mila nodded. Gracie took a hold of her hand and headed downstairs to find the house quiet and dark.

'Where is Papa?' Mila rubbed her eyes with her spare hand.

'I don't know, sweetie. Let's go find him.'

They peeked into every room downstairs. No lights. No movement. Even Luca's office was empty, though his laptop was whirring and his desk light was on as though he had stepped away for a moment, meaning to return.

Mila's bottom lip started to quiver.

'I think he's hiding,' Gracie said, her voice unnaturally bright. 'You know, hide-and-seek?'

Mila nodded slowly.

'We'll keep looking, OK?'

'OK.'

Gracie made a big play of turning on lights and leaping into rooms with a lot of noise as though hoping to catch him out. She had managed to keep the girl entertained through tiredness, and through boredom, but she wasn't sure she would be able to tap-dance her way around Mila's father not being within shouting distance.

Heading down the expanse leading to the back door, Gracie switched on the light and did her biggest 'Ha!' to find Luca walking inside.

'Papa!' Mila called out, slipping out of Gracie's grasp and running to him. Luca held out his arms, and lifted her, cuddling her against his large frame. As always, Gracie's breath caught at the sight. Father and daughter. Protector and innocent. It didn't seem like such a big ask to want the same relationship with her own father.

But when Luca's dark gaze lifted, his intense expression was anything but protective. It slammed into hers, rooting her to the spot.

The words 'Good evening, Luca' stuck in Gracie's throat. They stood on either side of the foyer, simply staring at each other—Luca running a hand over Mila's curls, Gracie wringing her hands, denying herself the urge to tidy her sleep-ruffled hair.

'You didn't hide very well, Papa,' Mila said, unaware of the very adult undercurrents. 'We found you almost instantly.'

'Did you, now?' Luca asked, his voice low and ominous, his attention focused purely on Gracie.

Again Gracie felt the shift, but this was not from the remnants of any dream. Something *had* changed. Gracie could feel it in the air, which was so thick with significance she had to breathe deep of it to get any oxygen to her lungs. But she couldn't pinpoint the difference, just that it was…different.

Luca slipped Mila to the ground. 'Why don't you go see if Cat needs help with the vegetables?'

'OK.' Mila trotted off.

Luca strolled towards Gracie. Slowly. Deliberately. So much for Luca's protective nature; Gracie would not have felt less protected if she were standing before him naked. She swallowed and searched for something to say, anything that would erect a sudden wall between her and the mounting awareness that was slamming against her.

'You once said Mila looks very much like her mother,' she said, her words coming out in a rush. 'But I have not seen any pictures about the house.'

She could not have built a wall quicker if she tried. Luca stopped and his expression closed down. Gracie crossed her arms across her chest to shield herself from the sudden chill.

'She does look very like her mother,' he said slowly.

'And did you two know each other long before you married?' Her voice was still shrill but at least she had managed to put the brakes on the frantic pace of her words.

Luca's eyes narrowed. 'We had known each other from childhood. But let's not talk of that. I was wondering if you were feeling as suffocated as I am, being indoors with the glorious, cool night air beckoning us outside.' He motioned outdoors, which opened up before Gracie like a gaping black hole, as dark and impenetrable as his eyes.

Gracie ran her sweating palms down over her hips. 'Suffocated?' she repeated. 'No way. I'm cool as a cucumber.'

Gracie flinched in fright at the sudden noise of Mila clumping back into the room, trotting in circles around her father. 'Cat does not need my help,' Mila said. 'She has already put the vegetables in the dinner which will be ready in *un momento*.'

Gracie clapped her hands together in agreement, the sound sharp and echoing in the lofty room. 'Maybe the two of you should have dinner alone tonight. Mila has missed you today, so why don't you catch up? I'm pooped anyway, so I'll just head to bed. Alone. To sleep.' Gracie shot them two-thumbs-up. 'Cool bananas?'

Gracie backed towards the staircase as two pairs of dark eyes watched her in mirrored mystification. She sent Mila an air-kiss, had a moment of pure panic when she thought Luca might think it was for him, then gave up and took off up the stairs two at a time, only stopping once she was in her room with the door closed.

Moonlight spilled through her French windows, beckoning her outside. She ran towards the light, shoving the windows open with a clang then gulped in great measures of the invigorating night air which she had only just told Luca she had no need for.

She grabbed hold of the cool concrete balustrade, the scrape of her fingernails rasping across the rough expanse doing little to alleviate the flood of images sluicing through her mind.

The blinding truth, the shift, the change was that now she knew the situation was more grave than just her having a crush on Luca. There was something more between them. There had been since the first moment their eyes had locked. There had been that rare zing of unquestionably mutual interest, which had led to some fast and furious flirtation. Then somehow, when Gracie wasn't paying attention, a switch had been flipped and flirtation had become temptation. She had tried to ignore it, hoping it would die a natural death. But it had only evolved.

No woman could look upon him without a hint of a knee wobble. She had her excuse. But what about him?

He was a man who had lost his wife a year before, and had lived in his country manor with his daughter clamped to his side ever since. Unless he had been dallying with one of the staff or, just as unlikely, with a regularly visiting sister-in-law, he could very well have been abstinent for all that time.

There. That was it. She was a red-blooded female. A stranger who would be out of his home, out of his country and out of his life soon enough, so he was having ideas.

Strangely, Gracie felt much better with this theory than with the other that had been flitting simultaneously through her head. What if she was developing real feelings for a flesh-and-blood Italian man? Just as her mother had before her.

She buried her head in her hands and let out a great, awful groan. Would the Lane women never learn?

Gracie slept fitfully that night, constantly imagining a knock at her door that never came.

She had felt almost desperate enough to pack her bags and sneak out the back door halfway through the night, but that was never really an option. She had no money, no other friends in Rome, nowhere else to turn. And it would have been too hurtful to leave Mila in the lurch like that, with no explanations, no goodbyes.

The fact that it would have also meant leaving Mila's father couldn't come into the equation. She had to resist her own urges, and the promises hidden just below the surface of his warm gaze. And she would do it by keeping her mother's constant disappointment in herself at indulging in her own Italian liaison ringing through her head as a mantra.

After an early cold shower, Gracie found Mila in her room already playing with her toys.

'Good morning, Gracie,' Mila said.

'Good morning, sweetheart. Did you have a nice dinner last night?' Gracie asked.

'I did. It was just Papa and me,' she said, puffing out her chest. Mila then kept chattering away to Pino in Italian, her voice lilting and tripping across the words, giving the old language such sweetness.

Gracie's throat constricted. This little girl, the miniature version of herself, was so far under her skin already she was concerned that when the time came to leave, there would be more than one person hurt by the parting.

'Did you eat anything nice last night?' Gracie asked.

'We did,' Mila said. 'I ate *all* of Papa's *gelato*. But he has gone away so it will be just the two of us tonight.' She said it with such a stiff upper lip Gracie knew she was copying her father's words.

But Luca was gone? Gone where? Why? Had she done something wrong? Had it something to do with the unacceptable electricity that had arced between them the night before? Gracie licked her lips and knew there was no way she could bombard a four-year-old with such questions.

'He had work to do in the city,' Mila continued. 'And since you and Gran-nonna and Cat can look after me, I told him it was all right with me.'

Well, there you go. Work. He had work to do. Grannonna had predicted that Gracie being in the house with Mila would give Luca a chance to revert to lion status once more.

Well, bully for him, Gracie thought, feeling somewhat uncharitable about being left behind...to do *her* job. She was thinking herself in circles when what she should have been doing was teaching Mila. Only then could she expect Luca to live up to his side of the bargain.

'I was thinking we could learn all about Australia today. I would put money on the fact that you have no idea what a billabong, a doona and a kelpie are.'

Mila stopped playing with Pino and listened intently, just as Gracie had expected she would.

Luca drove into Rome himself. He needed the peace of the open road, the sanctuary of his smooth driving car, and he needed the time alone to think.

He'd told Mila he was going into work, and he was. His people there would probably fall over from the shock of seeing him in the flesh for the first time in almost a year.

He had called home from his car phone twice to talk to Cat, making sure Mila was OK. The first time she had been playing with Pino in her room; the second time Cat reported that Gracie had been teaching Mila a song about 'a pub with no beer'. He had laughed down the phone with such vigour he had stunned Cat into silence.

He could have asked for Gracie but the truth was he had no idea what to say to her. Their parting the night before had been odd, fraught with a powerful and staggering tension. He barely understood why he had been so on edge, so deciphering *her* motives had been entirely beyond him.

Women were a species unto themselves. Mila amazed him every minute of the day with her courage and intelligence. Gran-nonna talked in riddles so often he wasn't entirely certain she wasn't going quietly senile. Jemma had the capacity to continue visiting, even though her own parents had demanded she put a stop to it.

But Gracie was something else again. He never knew if the woman was revealing parts of herself she had never shown to another soul, or if she was talking him in circles in order to distance him. And now, since she had come bursting into his home and his life, he was looking over his relationship with Sarina with a fresh eye, and wondering if he had ever really known *her* as well as he had thought he had.

He *would* show his face at work, but he had specifically come to Rome that day for another purpose. His gears crunched as he downshifted before turning his car into a street in a less affluent area on the outskirts of Rome. He slowed then switched off the engine and a mismatched family of cats scuttled across the road and behind a row of dented dustbins.

After he locked his car, checking twice that the alarm was set, he found the run-down apartment block he was looking for. The whitewash was long since sparkling, showcasing centuries-old stone beneath, and the front security door hung at an odd angle from its one remaining hinge.

He had pulled just about every favour owing to him to find this place. He had rebuilt several bridges in the process, shocking old clients and colleagues by calling on them for the first time in months. And finally, one of his old friends in a high-up government position had come through with the goods.

Luca looked up, his eyes scanning over washing lines hanging between the buildings a couple of floors above. *This* was the last known residence of Antonio Graziano? If so, he was glad he had come on his own first.

Despite the underwhelming welcome, Luca ran up the front steps and entered. The old open-grille lift looked life-threatening, so he took the stairs to the top floor. Once there, he gave himself one last chance to back away. Finding Gracie's father, which had started out as a means to an end, now meant something else. It meant bringing about a completely different end. Once Gracie's father was found, Gracie would leave. It was a simple equation with unexpectedly complicated consequences. Jemma was right; it was best dealt with sooner rather than later. Before Mila became too attached. And before he…

Luca shook the thoughts from his head and pounded on the apartment door.

*   *   *

By ten o'clock that night the Siracusa house had come alive with the sound of its lord and master returning home.

Though it had been difficult to get her down, Mila had finally fallen asleep, safe in the knowledge that of course her father would come in to kiss her as soon as he got home.

Gracie stretched her ears to hear his footsteps bound up the stairs. She heard Mila's door creak open and moments later there came the back-and-forth murmur of a sleepy voice and a soft, deep voice as daughter and father said goodnight.

After silence had reigned for a couple of minutes, she heard Mila's door close and Luca's footsteps fade away.

She went back to her book, an English version of John Christopher's *The Prince in Waiting* she had found in the library, but even though it was one of her childhood favourites, she had not been able to lose herself in it.

A whole day had gone by since she had fled from Luca like a confused teenager and she knew she had to make contact again, to get their working relationship back on an even footing or it would only make for even more unpleasant days ahead. She knew just where to find him.

Dressed in a newly washed tracksuit, a long-sleeved top and her ubiquitous bed socks, Gracie pushed open the French windows and stepped onto the upstairs balcony. There he was, leaning on the concrete balustrade, staring across the grounds of the estate, which were lit by patches of silvery moonlight.

Dressed in charcoal suit trousers and a pale blue business shirt rolled up to the elbows, he looked utterly devastating. She padded towards him and pinched herself to hold back the desire to reach out and fix the one half of his collar which was adorably crooked.

'Hello, Luca,' Gracie said, her voice captured and carried by the late-night breeze.

Luca turned to her, his face shrouded by darkness. 'Good evening.'

She joined him, leaning on the balustrade, but several feet away.

'How was work?' When he didn't answer, Gracie resorted to baiting him. If it worked on his daughter... 'Is the lion back on his throne?'

He glanced her way, his eyes crinkling in budding delight. 'The lion?'

'Mmm.' Gracie edged closer. 'Gran-nonna said you were once a *lion* in the world of high finance.'

He grimaced. 'And that I had since become a house cat?'

'Well, not in so many words...'

'But that's what she meant. And she's right. I have spent far too long away from my post.'

'And after today, now you have returned to your scratching post...?' She swiped a paw at him, growling like a lion cub.

Luca laughed. He stood up straight, stretching his long, sinewy arms behind his head. 'I suppose the lion has awakened from his slumber.' His glance soon switched into full-attention mode. 'And I have you to thank for that.'

Her swiping paw degenerated into a wobbly hand. 'Phooey. I have done nothing out of the ordinary.'

'Yes. You have. The only change in my situation in the last twelve months has been you. Without you looking out for Mila, I would not have been disposed to head back to town on my own. For that I will be forever grateful.'

Gracie took the compliment. She gave him a little nod to acknowledge lest it decay into a 'no I'm not', 'yes, you are' type conversation. She leant her elbows against the wall and looked out over the grounds. 'So your trip to Rome was a success?'

Luca turned away to face the grounds as well. He listened hard to hear the babbling creek in the far distance but he could not hear a thing above his own hard-beating heart.

That was the question of the hour. Had he achieved what he had set out to achieve in Rome? He had gone to Rome to catch up at work, so yes. He had gone to Rome to find the whereabouts of Gracie's father, so yes. Though circumstances meant he was not ready to let her in on that titbit. Not yet.

But he had gone for other reasons more close to home as well. He had gone to see if the time away from Mila hurt too much to bear. He had missed his Mila but he knew it was in her best interests that he gave her some space. It had been easier, and more fulfilling than he had expected, because he knew it had been the right thing to do.

But he'd had unexpected results as well. Where he had found the thought of his daughter safe at home consoling, liberating even, leaving another house member had been a different matter. Even once he had left her father's apartment, his mind had strayed to Gracie all day.

During his meetings at work, he had missed her smart mouth. He had imagined the humour with which she would have reprimanded his colleagues who had grown soft in his absence. He missed her honest face, which would have warned him the minute he sounded sanctimonious. He missed her warm body filling the space next to him on the lounge chair. He missed that most of all.

'I'm not exactly sure,' he finally said, answering Gracie's question. He felt her watching him, her bottomless blue eyes seeking out the answers in his body language which he would not give verbally. He stood up, tucked his hands deep within his trouser pockets and offered her no more insight than a drowsy smile. 'It's been a big day. I am going to turn in.'

'Of course.'

'Goodnight, Gracie.'

'Goodnight, Luca.'

His name drifted to him on a sigh and it gave him pause. Giving in, he walked to her, leant in and placed a lingering kiss on her cheek. Her skin felt as soft and warm against his unshaven face as he had imagined it would.

She smelled of freshly laundered cotton and lemon *gelato*. He gave into the urge to drink in her scent as he pulled away. Her eyes slowly flittered open. He looked upon her for several seconds more before commanding his feet to take him away from her.

CHAPTER SEVEN

GRACIE and Mila were in the middle of a tea party with Pino the plastic palomino during playtime Tuesday morning, when a raucous noise from downstairs caught their attention. Voices laughing and squealing, and Caesar barking the house down, were enough inducement for Mila to canter out of her room and around the corner before Gracie even knew what was happening. It took her longer to drag her older bones from the floor. She followed at a more sensible walk.

She made it to the top of the stairs in time to see Mila leap from the bottom step and into the arms of a stocky, unshaven hunk decked out in leather and denim with a couple of well-worn travel bags slung over his shoulder. The hunk slid Mila to the floor and knelt down to give Caesar a great wrestling hug. Cat and other staff stood by and watched, their faces filled with glee.

'Gracie! Gracie!' Mila called out from behind the gent's legs. 'Zio Domenico has come home!'

Funny, she thought, *Luca has never mentioned a brother, and in this tight little clan that seems odd.*

She made it to the bottom of the stairs by the time the hunk swivelled around to see who Mila was talking to. She slowed, stuck one hand in the back pocket of her jeans and stepped forward, right hand outstretched.

'Uncle Domenico, I take it?'

He gave her a brief nod. 'Call me Dom.'

'I'm Gracie Lane. Australian. Tourist. Mila's new English tutor.'

His experienced gaze raked over her form, decked out in slim-fit jeans and a red V-necked sweater that had seen better days, finishing up at her bare feet. He finally took her outstretched hand and planted a lingering kiss upon her wrist. 'It is my distinct pleasure to meet *you*.'

Gracie almost laughed aloud at his cockiness. She stepped back to put some space between herself and the practised Lothario.

He turned back to Mila, who was bouncing up and down at his side. 'Why was I not informed of this new addition to our little household?'

Mila giggled and twirled and said, 'Because you are never around long enough for it to matter.'

Domenico let go a great bellowing laugh. 'I wonder where she picked *that* one up from? So where *is* my big brother? I am surprised he did not follow in the little one's wake.'

'He's working, I guess,' Gracie said.

Domenico took a moment to compute this information. 'Working? Really?' He shot a glance at the half-open door to Luca's office. 'Best not disturb him, then.' He hitched his bags more comfortably onto his shoulder. 'Come, my little kitty Cat. Bring me coffee. I will need to lubricate my vocal cords before tonight's episode of the Adventures of Domenico Siracusa.'

Dom grabbed Mila around the waist and slung her over his shoulder, kicking and squealing. As he disappeared up the stairs, the staff and the dog followed in his energetic wake. But the one person in the house who had not come out of his nearby cave was Luca. Gracie looked over to his office door. Several moments after the circus died down to its usual peaceful stillness the clatter of his keyboard started up again.

She took in a deep breath, remembering the way he had

kissed her cheek the night before, his stubble rasping against her skin, creating shivers through her body that had returned over and over through the night. The damn thing had been entirely platonic, yet what did that matter? She had woken up with the same warm languor of the day before, though this time she could remember every second of the dreams that had made her feel so delicious.

Gracie sauntered over to Luca's door. She had hoped she would be able to start a natural conversation without babbling like an idiot, and, thankfully, circumstances had given her the perfect opener. She knocked. The keyboard clatter stopped.

'*Entrato,*' he said.

Gracie pushed the door open but lingered in the doorway of the lion's den. Luca was not a happy camper; she could all but see the storm clouds gathering above his head as he frowned irritably at his computer.

'How you can work through such a commotion, I'll never know,' she said.

He barely gave her a glance and, even then, his only words were, 'Where is Mila?'

O...K...

Gracie entered and took up residence on his couch. 'Some strange young guy I've never seen before stole her away from me.'

Luca went back to punching indiscriminately at his keyboard. 'So you met my younger brother.'

'It seems I did. Funny, I didn't even know you had a brother. He lives here?'

'Off and on.' Luca pressed a finger down on one keyboard button and Gracie was pretty sure he was deleting everything he had just typed.

'Do you guys hate each other or what?'

Luca finally looked her in the eye. After staring her down for a few moments, he slipped his hands from the keyboard. His beautiful lips had almost disappeared, the line of his mouth was so tight. 'He is my flesh and blood.'

'That's no answer,' she said. First there had been no mention that Domenico existed, and now Luca was bristling like a threatened echidna. 'You can choose your friends…' she began, but Luca gave her nothing. He just stared at his fingernails, which were digging into the edge of his desk.

'He is charming, no?' Luca asked. He shot her a quick look from beneath his sooty lashes. His dark gaze had a dangerous edge Gracie had not seen before. She had to swallow so that her voice would come out normally.

'I guess he is. He kissed my hand like I was some princess, if that's what you mean.' Gracie knew her bemusement came through in her voice, and she knew Luca had heard it too.

He shifted an elbow to the table and leant his chin upon his knuckles, his sombre face softening as the beginning of a smile tugged at his mouth. 'He didn't turn your head, then?'

Gracie blinked back at him. 'Please! I know you've only known me for a few days, but did you actually imagine I would become some quivering girly girl at Domenico's feet? I may be a tourist, but I'm no hick. I can see slick coming at me from a mile away.'

Luca watched her a few moments longer, his eyes bright and lively, his enduring smile warming her from the inside out. No, Luca's younger brother had not turned her head. She knew all too well what that felt like, and Luca's younger brother had not even shown up on her radar. Her radar was already beeping loud enough because of one disarming Siracusa, and one Siracusa male was plenty, and too much, all at once.

Then suddenly it occurred to Gracie why Luca had been so bristly, why he had not come out of his room, why she had been subjected to twenty questions. *Was he actually jealous?*

She shot up off the couch. 'I'd better go check on Mila. We were making some real breakthroughs.' *If pat-a-cake, pat-a-cake could be considered a breakthrough...* 'See you at dinner.'

'Mmm,' Luca hummed, sending goose-pimples over Gracie's skin. 'That you will.'

Gracie hotfooted it from the room and up the stairs. For the first time in all the comings and goings since she had arrived, there was another man in the house, and the testosterone level had quadrupled.

This was going to be some night.

Dinner was a riot.

Dom had the whole family in thrall with tales of his trip to Crete. The fact that he had barely escaped arrest, fistfights and ancient curses was apparently nothing new.

Dom's arrival had been enough to bring Gran-nonna out of her cottage. Grey-haired and sombrely dressed though she was, she so obviously adored her younger grandson's daredevil attitude. She watched wide-eyed as Dom stood atop his chair, wielding an unlit candelabrum as a prop.

On the other hand Luca's eyes rarely left his plate, and when they did flicker to his guests it was only to glower or ask someone to pass the salt. Gracie thought he was taking his big-brother attitude too far. Sure, Dom was a larrikin, but he had nothing tying him down, so why not?

When Dom's story ended and he plopped back into his

chair, fixing Gracie with a flirtatious stare, she was understandably caught unawares.

'Gracie, have you found yourself an Italian lover as yet?' he asked.

'Domenico, watch your mouth,' Gran-nonna chastised in her mother tongue, slapping him lightly behind his head, her grin weakening the impact of the reprimand.

Gracie looked around the table for an ally but Mila was busy singing to herself and Luca was watching her with as much interest as Dom, though still glowering all the same.

'What? It is a relevant question, no?' Dom asked, his face all innocence as he looked about the tableau of guests. 'Gracie is a beautiful woman. She is a tourist come to seek out the pleasures of our sumptuous country. And from what I have heard, Australian girls are not so shy as those from less…hot countries.'

She could have continued with her sideshow-clown impersonation, but she knew from Dom's cheeky smile that he was merely baiting the new girl for sport. With a practised glare piercing enough to have stopped men more determined than Dom in their tracks, Gracie pointed a finger in his direction. 'Any more of that type of talk and you'll be receiving an even stronger slap to the back of the head from me.'

Dom cowered and held up two hands in submission. 'No! Please. Anything but that.'

'You deserve nothing less,' Luca insisted, finally joining the conversation. 'In her brief stay with us, Gracie has done wonders with our little Mila. And for that she deserves our deepest respect.'

Gracie dragged her gaze to look at Luca, though she had a feeling she would later regret it. She had been expecting a cheeky glint to have finally reached his usually smiling eyes, but her host was deadly serious.

Luca held up his glass of red wine. 'To the kindness of strangers.'

The others at the table followed suit. Her inhibitions loosened by the classic Chianti, drawn from Luca's vineyard, Gracie stared in silence as Luca brought his glass to his mouth, that mouth that ought to have been immortalised in marble, and took a prolonged sip of his wine, his warm, expressive gaze never leaving her once.

All of a sudden, Mila's Pino trotted too close to her water glass and knocked it over, spilling the contents over the lace tablecloth. 'Hell's bells!' Mila shouted in perfect English.

'Whoa!' Dom yelled, his laughter echoing through the room. Cat raced to the scene, mopping up the innocuous spill with Mila's napkin, and crossing herself repeatedly as she did so.

Gracie's hand shot to her mouth. She knew there was only one place Mila would have learnt such an English term as that: from her English tutor.

'I am so sorry,' she gushed, her cheeks heating instantly. 'She must have picked that one up from me.'

'Don't worry yourself, Gracie,' Dom insisted. 'Mila is too sheltered. Let her have some fun. Let her live a little.'

If Luca had told Dom where to go she would not have been surprised, in fact she would not have even stopped him. But he did not. He sipped on his drink and kept his mouth shut. Since Dom's arrival it was as if the house had fallen into the twilight zone.

Gracie gave a little shrug. 'Nevertheless, I promise to be more careful.'

Gran-nonna stood and laid her napkin on the table. 'Perhaps now we should retire to the sitting room.'

Dom stood and copied her move, puffing out his chest, acting terribly regal although with his stubble and his dishevelled haircut he didn't quite pull it off. 'Yes,' he said, 'let's.'

He held out an elbow and Gran-nonna placed her slim hand in the crook, escorting her cheeky grandson into the sitting room.

Mila had had enough of being fussed over by Cat so she slithered from her chair and cantered after her uncle and great-grandmother. Cat cleared several plates and left through a side-door into the kitchen beyond, leaving Luca and Gracie alone in the loaded silence.

Gracie felt as if she did not know where to put her hands. She scraped back her chair, her napkin fell from her lap to the floor, she bent to pick it up, placed it on the table with as much finesse as she could muster, then on considerably wobbly legs walked to Luca's side.

'I truly am sorry about Mila's outburst. I've lived away from home so long I no longer have to watch my mouth.'

Luca placed his napkin on the table and stood by her. 'Don't worry about it, Gracie. I trust your instincts with Mila.'

'But why?' she blurted out, proving she couldn't control her mouth still. 'I've only been here a few days and I have already managed to teach Mila at least one new swear word.'

Luca's mouth stirred into a crooked smile. 'And in that same amount of time I have learnt some new English terms myself. I have no doubt that my decision to bring you into my home was one of the finest I have ever made.'

Gracie had enough Dutch courage to bring up that other thing. The attraction between them. The chemistry. The awareness. Whatever one wanted to call it. The heat that wouldn't die down even after an ice-cold shower. If she was to remain in his home for any prolonged amount of time, it would have to be addressed.

'Luca, there is more to my concern.'

'I know,' he said. 'Please don't think I have forgotten about my side of the bargain.'

Bargain?

'Even with the constant state of flux in this household I have not forgotten about your father.'

Oh! Gracie was mortified that, in all her muddled confusion about the infatuation she was developing, the most important thing in the world to her had managed to slip down her to-do list with such ease.

'I didn't want to say anything until I knew more,' Luca continued, 'but I can tell that, despite your cheerful countenance, this has been weighing on you a great deal. I have already put out some preliminary feelers and am awaiting a satisfactory conclusion before I go any further. I promise as soon as I know anything more, you will know the same.'

Gracie couldn't believe her ears, and was angry with herself for thinking that he had forgotten, or didn't care. The hug that she had been so good in withholding in Rome would not be stopped. She threw herself into his arms, standing on tiptoe so she could wrap her hands about his shoulders and bury her face against his neck. 'Thank you, Luca. Thank you so much.'

After a brief moment, Luca's arms wrapped about her as well, his hands sliding along her back until they tucked tidily along her waist. Once ensconced in his full embrace, Gracie discovered that the length and breadth of him fitted against her all too perfectly. Her soft bits sank against his hard bits as if they had been made for precisely that purpose.

Luca cleared his throat in the silence and Gracie leapt away from him.

'Sorry,' she said, her voice breathless. 'I mean. Thanks. Really, thank you for trying.' She reached out and gave his arm a chummy punch.

Luca watched her in silence for several moments and Gracie wished she could wind back the clock, not drink a drop of Chianti, not throw herself at her host and then not chuff him on the arm.

But, gentleman that he was, Luca made no mention of her apparent case of foot-in-mouth disease. He just smiled tenderly and held out his arm. 'Time we joined the others?'

Somehow, Gracie could not muster the wherewithal to place her arm through his. She just stood before him, staring at the top button of his shirt, biting at her lip. So Luca took her hand, laced it through his arm, placed a warm, reassuring hand over hers and led her towards the sitting room, where Gran-nonna was playing a lively song on the piano. Dom had obviously chosen the song, as he was up dancing, with Mila bobbing on his hip.

The first moment she could, Gracie slipped out of Luca's hold and made a beeline for a comfortable spot on the sofa within reaching distance of a glass of local grappa. Luca sauntered up behind the couch, leaning his forearms against the chair back. If she moved a fraction to the right, his fingers would be entangled in her hair.

'I was like him once,' Luca said so quietly Gracie was not sure it was meant for her ears.

She took a fortifying sip of her drink. 'You were *never* like him.'

Luca turned to face her, and blinked, and she knew he had been in his own world. But he finally laughed, the sound warm and smooth, his smile full of secrets Gracie itched tò have him tell. 'Believe what you wish, *bella*.'

Luca turned to watch his family, but Gracie watched Luca. She fought the urge to reach out and run a finger along the line of his strong jaw, to test if it was as warm as she imagined it would be or if it was as cool as the exquisite marble statues he looked so like.

Only when the song finished did Dom and Mila realise they had company. 'Finally!' Dom said. 'We thought you two had decided to have your own little party without us, didn't we, Mila?'

'No,' Mila insisted. 'I knew Papa would come for me.'

Gran-nonna rose slowly from the piano stool and hobbled over to sit in a wing chair, where she sipped on her own glass of grappa.

'Play for me, Papa,' Mila insisted, seeing the piano stool was now empty. She wriggled from Dom's embrace and ran to Luca, tugging him on the hand with all her might.

Luca shot Gracie a swift, preoccupied glance. 'Not tonight, Mila.'

Mila, clever kid that she was, followed his line of sight. 'Gracie won't mind,' Mila insisted. 'Play for her. Show her how cool you are on the piano.'

Gracie winked at the little one in an effort to ease the grim look on her face.

Realising he was no longer the centre of attention, Dom bounded across the room and sat beside her. 'Yeah, come on, Luca. Show Gracie how *cool* you are.' He laid a hand on her knee, and she just as smoothly shifted it away.

At Gracie's effortless dismissal of Dom's varied charms, Luca's eyes narrowed and his lips stretched into the unhurried smile that always made her chest clench.

He let Mila drag him to the piano. He took a seat then

lifted Mila to sit on the chair next to him. She lifted the wooden cover, but was so small Luca had to help her raise it the final few inches. He cracked his knuckles; Mila copied. He rested his hands atop the keys; Mila copied.

Though they must have seen it a trillion times, Dom and Gran-nonna both watched with such easy smiles. While Gracie felt so overwhelmed by all of the devotion in the room, she could barely take a breath.

Then Luca began to play, brilliantly. It was a playful piece that Gracie recognised, though more likely from a copycat TV jingle than from the opera from whence it had originally come. She slipped down in the chair until her head rested against its back. The grappa, the Chianti and the music combined to make her feel warm and snuggly.

Not able to properly contribute, Mila eventually slipped off the chair and spun around and around on the spot until her great-grandmother took her in hand so she wouldn't crash into the furniture.

Gracie felt Dom lean back into the chair beside her.

'Where did he learn to do that?' she asked, her gaze remaining on his elder brother.

'Self-taught,' Dom said, trying once more to slide a hand onto her knee.

Gracie picked it up with as much enthusiasm as if it were a dead fish and dropped it on his lap. 'I thought all Italians were meant to be exceedingly polite.'

'And I thought all Australian girls were tall and tanned,' Dom said.

Gracie coughed out a laugh. 'Cheeky beast,' she said between clenched teeth then looked across to make sure Mila hadn't heard. But Mila was happily sitting on Gran-nonna's lap, trying to lick the remnants from her grappa glass.

'I am half-Italian,' Gracie explained. 'As are thousands of Australians.' Gracie hoped she didn't sound as defensive as she felt.

'Yet you're not a bit polite,' Dom said. 'I guess we are both not what we seem.'

He was probably right. She saw him as an incorrigible flirt, ripe for a fling. Back home, he was exactly the kind of man she would look twice at—cute, loud and dangerous. Yet now she knew that his sort was utterly harmless. Luca was infinitely more dangerous. You could control a relationship if it was all about fun, and laughter, and teasing, and baiting. But she and Luca had so very quickly developed past that.

She closed her eyes, soaking in Luca's deft touch on the piano keys. 'He's really good,' she said, unable to hide her affectionate sigh.

'That he is,' Dom agreed. 'A man of many talents.'

Did she hear an echo of bitterness in that statement? She turned to face Dom and shot him a winning smile. 'Do go on.'

Knowing he had been sprung, Dom grinned back. 'Did you know he won a bravery award for rescuing the local fire chief's Dalmatian from a flooding river when he was nine?'

Gran-nonna's first words to her filtered through her wine-fizzled brain. 'Thus leading to his wish to start a home for lost dogs, right?'

Dom was obviously impressed. 'I see I am going to have to do better than that.' He brought a hand to his stubbly chin and looked suitably pensive. 'Did you know that Luca's mortgage company is one of the top ten earners in the country?' He held up a finger to shush her. 'But that it provides more interest-free loans to low-income families than any company above it on the list?'

Gracie saw a pattern fast forming. 'How does one possibly live in the shadow of a brother such as this?'

Dom nodded slowly and shrugged, mocking himself all the while. 'But wait,' he said, 'there's more. Did you know that he was married to a woman who did not love him, all to save the woman, her family and his family from his brother's disgrace?'

'I did not know that either,' Gracie said before the words actually sank in. Every ounce of comfort the grappa had given her evaporated as a sudden chill licked her body. Gracie shuffled her bottom back in the seat until she was upright.

'Disgrace?' she repeated.

She saw the swift shadow of hurt flash across Dom's brown eyes, paler, unhappier versions of his brother's. Her voice came out as a soft whisper, only loud enough for Dom's ears. 'Are you saying Luca married Sarina because she was pregnant?'

Dom nodded, his movements suddenly laboured. And the whole story came into brilliant, clear focus.

'With your child?' she asked, already knowing the answer.

He kept nodding.

'You mean that Mila is not even his daughter?'

The song finished and Gracie's head swung back to find Luca watching her with that same dark, ominous expression that had clouded his usually composed features from the moment Dom had returned home.

All that glowering and bristling suddenly made perfect sense.

CHAPTER EIGHT

THE small party broke up soon after. Gran-nonna retired to her cottage. Dom claimed hours of unpacking to do in order to locate his toothbrush. And Luca took a sleeping Mila to her room.

Gracie begged a need to stay in the warm candlelit room a while longer, and when alone she remained on the couch, studying a photograph of Luca and Mila that resided on the side-table.

Mila was only a baby, maybe only a couple of months old. Her eyes were the same bright blue, but her dark hair had not yet grown. Luca's hair was shorter then, and he hadn't shaved in several days. They were cheek to cheek. Both grinning. Luca looked down the barrel of the camera while Mila was looking to someone off to the side. Her mother, Gracie figured. She could see without a doubt that Luca was sublimely happy. Whether Mila was his natural daughter or not, he loved her.

Gracie's heart ripped right down the middle. The picture was so poignant, as it represented Luca and Mila in a perfect world. A perfect bubble of happiness. If they could live in that photograph forever the two of them would never want for anything, or anyone else.

Yet it never really had been perfect. It had been crazed from the outset. When Sarina had died, speeding towards the nightlife she so craved, the bubble had shown its first true crack. And now Mila was growing older, full of questions, and Gracie knew that Dom felt guilty and bitter about the situation. Not only was the bubble not perfect, but it was also ripe to burst.

Half an hour later Gracie trudged up to her room, passing Mila's open bedroom door on the way. The young girl had obviously had a second wind. She sat cross-legged on the floor with Luca sitting the same way, and she was teaching him pat-a-cake, pat-a-cake with invisible mud just as Gracie had taught it to her.

Gracie could tell Luca was tired, his shoulders were slumped and he kept trying to hide his yawns. But so long as Mila was willing and able to share her time, he was not complaining.

She looked from Luca to Mila. The way he deferred to her in any conversation, the way he patted her hair whenever she became distressed, the way he looked at her with such unconditional love. No one would ever think they weren't father and daughter. And, though Gracie had no real first-hand experience of how a father and daughter ought to be, she thought from the moment she had seen these two together that this was as good as it could get.

Gracie's thoughts turned to her stepfather, the man who married her mother when Gracie had been fifteen. The man who co-produced two perfect blonde, lanky, bronzed Aussie kids within the next few years. Kids that Gracie barely knew, as she had moved out of home the day she finished high school. Her stepfather, who at her mother's funeral had produced an Italian passport so that if one day she went in search of her real father it would make the mission easier, knowing it would help her feel less as if her whole world had been whipped from under her.

And somewhere out there lived her actual father. She felt wretchedly selfish that, no matter that her stepfather was a good man, she needed more. She needed to know exactly where she came from before she had any chance of figuring out where she was going.

And would this adorable, blissful little girl one day feel the same way? Gracie's heart felt as if it was tearing from her chest. And she didn't know who she felt more frightened for, Mila or Luca.

Something akin to a sob caught Luca's attention. He turned to face the door, his hands stopping mid-pat-a-cake.

Gracie was standing in the doorway, leaning her head against her hand, which was wrapped tight around the doorframe. Her large blue eyes shimmered in the low light.

'Hi,' he said.

'Hi,' she said back, her voice drifting across the room in a strange whisper.

Beside him Mila gave a great squeaking yawn, which broke the stranglehold of silence. Gracie peeled herself away from the door.

'Aren't you sleepy yet, Mila?' she asked.

Mila nodded. 'But I had to teach Papa how to play or else I would never have gone to sleep.'

His little girl's eyes blinked heavily, utterly negating her statement. God, how he loved her. He loved her so much his heart couldn't contain it. He reached out and brushed a curl from her sweet, flushed face.

'I see,' Gracie said, now standing behind him. 'And has Papa learnt?'

Luca stood, brushed his crushed trousers smooth and answered her raised eyebrow with a nod.

'Good,' she said. 'Bedtime for everyone.'

Mila held up her arms so that Gracie would rid her of her dress. It was obvious that she expected it of Gracie, not of him. And it had never been that way. Ever. It had always been him and Mila. Even when Gran-nonna was about. Even when Dom was home. Even when Sarina was alive. It had always been him and his little Mila against the world. And somehow this stranger had wandered aimlessly into their lives, and his little Mila was giving her love to another.

But wasn't that exactly what he wanted? To prepare her for school, and the big wide world and so on? To prepare her for life without him? To allow her to give herself to future friends and boyfriends without qualms that poor old Papa would not survive it?

Seeing her standing there, prepared for Gracie to get her ready for bed, he wondered if he would even survive this first concrete step in her emancipation.

As though Gracie sensed his reaction, she hesitated. Luca took a step back. 'Go ahead, please.'

Gracie blithely did as she was told. She pulled Mila's dress over her head, laying it neatly across the rocking-horse in the corner. Knowing exactly which drawer to go to, she pulled out Mila's favourite much-washed white nightie and pulled it over her head. Cooing all the while, Gracie then took the sleepy child to bed, helping her under the covers, kissing her forehead then whispering something in her ear that made the little one smile before she finally dropped off into the sleep of the innocent.

Luca held out an arm to let Gracie pass. The agonised look she shot him from beneath her dark lashes was not one he had seen before, so he could not take its measure. But it disturbed him all the same.

Who was he kidding? She disturbed him whether she was watching him from beneath her lashes, or if she ignored him completely whilst talking to his brother. She disturbed him even when she wasn't in the same room. Sure, he had achieved a mountain of work over the weekend, but if his mind had not wandered to wondering where she was and what she was doing every five minutes, he could have achieved a whole mountain range of work.

As they walked down the hall, side by side, Luca found the silence improbably oppressing. He felt like someone on a first date, leading a woman back to her apartment door, lost in the thought of whether or not a kiss would follow.

But this was no first date.

He risked a sideways glance. She was a million miles away. He could tell because her feet were scuffing the floor and she was nibbling at her inner cheek.

With her glossy curls raked back in a loose pony-tail, he had a good view of her profile. Her cheeks were still pink from the fire downstairs. Her dark eyelashes swept slowly to her cheek and back again as she blinked over and over again. In her regular get-up of an old T-shirt— this one advertising Melbourne Zoo—and jeans, she looked adorable. Her petite frame filled out her oft-washed clothes in such a manner he did not know whether she was an unsophisticated girl next door whom he wanted to safeguard, or a free spirit who was too wild for even him to tame. Though the former appealed to him more than he cared to admit, he feared it was the latter. The way she had clicked so easily with Dom only made that possibility all the greater. The fact was she had him baffled. Especially since he did not know why he cared so much either way.

Once they reached her bedroom door she stopped and turned. Her blue eyes were stormy. Something was worrying her to distraction.

'Sleepy?' he asked, sensing that she was no closer to sleep than he was.

She gave a quick shrug, her eyes flickering to his and away again. 'Not really.'

'How does hot chocolate sound?'

She fixed him with unblinking eyes as she tried to determine…something. 'Pretty good actually.'

Luca nodded shortly. 'How about I meet you on the balcony in ten minutes? I'll bring the drinks, you bring the chairs.'

Her cheek-nibbling efforts doubled. But finally she nodded, then stepped inside her room and softly shut the door.

And though it was certainly no first date, Luca felt the disappointment deep within him that he had missed out on his kiss.

Gracie leant on the inside of her bedroom door and breathed out most of her tension. Hot chocolate at midnight. With Luca. On the balcony. In the moonlight. With nothing but the owls to chaperon her.

Any other night, Gracie would have chastised herself incessantly to agreeing to such a thing, knowing that she would only fantasise about test-driving those gorgeous lips of his. But tonight her affections were tempered by the news that Luca was not Mila's natural father. There was no way she could go to sleep without talking it over with him. He would soon know something was wrong. When dealing at blackjack she never checked her face-down card, as the entire table would easily decipher what she had.

Three minutes had passed already. Gracie ran to the centre of her room. To change or not to change? To change. She whipped off her T-shirt and jeans, changed into black yoga tights, a black bedtime T-shirt and her pink bed socks.

She grabbed the first of the wrought-iron balloon-backed chairs from her suite and dragged it outside. When she returned with the second, Luca had arrived with a folding table and a Thermos of hot chocolate, and he was still dressed like an adult, not like a teenager at a boy-girl slumber party.

'Where is your Chocoholics Anonymous shirt?' he asked.

She had somehow hoped that he had been paying no attention that first morning on the balcony, considering he had never mentioned it since. But by the cheeky glint in his eye, she knew he had been paying very close attention.

'The Chocoholics Anonymous T-shirt has been retired,' she said with a warning tone in her voice.

'I am sorry to hear that.' He gave her an understanding smile. 'But I still feel overdressed.'

'I can lend you some bed socks if that would help.'

He glanced down at her feet, his smile widening as he took in her old, worn socks. The small crease appeared above his nose as he frowned. 'You know, I don't re-member ever seeing your feet in shoes. Always socks or nothing.'

'I like to feel the ground beneath my feet.' Gracie scrunched her toes into the tiles to remind herself that was where she wanted to stay. No use floating up onto cloud nine because Luca was giving her his whole range of smiles.

She took a seat and Luca followed suit. He filled two aluminium mugs with the steaming hot chocolate. She lifted her feet up to rest in the crook of the balustrade and, after grabbing a mug, wrapped her arms about her knees. 'Kelly and Cara would go mad for this place.'

'Invite them.'

Gracie cast him a glance that said 'please!' 'Invite them to pop over to Italy for the weekend to see the view?'

Luca shrugged. 'Not for the weekend, then. But any time they come over, tell them they are free to visit. We have enough room, and any friend of yours…' He let Gracie finish the thought on her own.

'I haven't even called them to let them know I am here,' she admitted.

'But they must be out of their minds with worry!'

'Nah. They have other things on their minds right now. Both are madly in love and would only have to drag themselves away from their men's arms to talk to me.'

Gracie cast Luca a quick glance to find him now staring out over the grounds as well.

'You don't approve of their partners?' he asked, before taking a slow sip of his drink.

'Lord, yes! Simon and Adam are superb. Kelly and Cara are livin' the dream. There is just no use bothering them if I don't need to. They're used to me. I'm kind of the irresponsible one in the crew.'

'That can't be true.'

'Oh, it is.'

'Then the two of them must be saints.'

'Not saints, just focused. Together. With plans and goals. I'm the one who had a job rather than a career. I'm the only one who flew off to Rome on a whim without leaving a forwarding address.'

Luca turned so that his knees rested either side of her chair and she felt his protective warmth curl around her. 'Gracie, I can't let you be so hard on yourself. Do you think I would have put the care of my daughter in your hands if I did not believe you are a responsible woman?'

At mention of *his* daughter, Gracie's stomach tightened. 'Who knows? Perhaps you were at the end of your tether and if it wasn't me it would have been some other hapless, homeless woman.'

He shook his head and Gracie could not meet his eyes, knowing the intensity within would be too much for her to endure.

'It would only ever have been you. You have much innate kindness though you would for some reason make me think otherwise. I have seen you with my grandmother. I have seen you with Mila. I think you would do anything for them, even at your own expense. You are the kindest, most selfless person I have ever known.'

Gracie's skin tingled from her head to her toes. 'Dealing with people is not so hard. It's all smoke and mirrors. It's all about distraction. Watch my right hand do magic while my left hand feeds you your vegetables.'

'I don't think so, Gracie.'

'Believe it. Working in the high-rollers room, I had to deal with bigger kids than Mila on a nightly basis.'

Luca shook his head. 'I don't buy it. You may have picked up a few tricks along the way, but you are not playing Mila, you truly care for her.'

Gracie swallowed to give herself a moment. Of course she cared for Mila. But the question was, how much? She had known this broken family for only a few days, yet she cared for them more than she had ever meant to. Her heart cracked a little every day she spent with them, as every day was a day closer to leaving them.

She had to answer him before he wondered about the answer himself. 'I adore her, Luca,' she said with a casual shrug. 'Because she is adorable.'

'Mmm,' Luca said, seeming to back down, 'that she is.'

The hot chocolate, which should have warmed her innards and prepared her for sleep, was not doing its job. She gulped down the fast-cooling liquid and slid her feet to the floor, carefully tucking them away from Luca's legs. 'I think it's time I hit the hay.'

Luca blinked and his brow did its adorable furrowed thing, showing her vernacular was a little too obscure for him.

'Bedtime for Gracie,' she explained.

He gave her one short nod. 'I think I'll stay out here a while longer. You don't need your chairs?'

She backed away, shaking her head. 'Keep 'em. See you tomorrow.'

'Goodnight.'

She didn't know whether to just kiss him and get it out of her system, or blurt out she knew Mila was not his. And, since neither seemed like an appropriate response to a simple *goodnight*, she smiled grimly and went into her room, knowing that both options still lingered on her horizon.

After finally falling into a heavy dreamless sleep, Gracie awoke to the soft tinkle of piano keys in the distance.

With an exhausted groan, she slid out of bed, wrapped her blanket around her and poked her head into the doorway. The sound was definitely coming from downstairs.

She shuffled along the hall and down the stairs, the blanket dragging behind her, the sombre, heartbreaking notes luring her all the way. She reached the sitting room to find the door closed. Whoever was in there wanted to be left alone.

Tough. They had woken her, they were going to have to deal with her. Gracie opened the door and closed it softly behind her. No use waking the rest of the household.

She found Luca bent over the keys, a single candle atop the piano his only light. As she walked closer she saw why. He had no music. He was playing from memory. And it was not a happy memory. His eyes were clamped shut tight, a sheen of sweat glowed upon his forehead and his body swayed as his long fingers danced over the keys in a haunting rhythm.

Gracie shivered as goose-pimples sprang up over her body. She sat on the same couch she had been slumped into that evening and tucked her feet beneath her, wrapping her shivering body into a small ball.

Luca made the music seem absolutely effortless. Hunched over the beautiful instrument, he made it sing, the sound wafting to the rafters and back again, vibrating through Gracie's body. It must have permeated the whole house, but Gracie was the only one to stir. She figured the others must have been used to it.

But if they had heard it before they must have recognised this man was in pain. Nothing else could create such an intense mournful sound. He was up at three o'clock in the morning, playing a piano in the dark, for God's sake. Had none of them done anything about it? It occurred to her that maybe this had been going on for so long that they didn't even hear it any more.

As the song came to a natural and heart-wrenching conclusion, Gracie gave a great sigh, which echoed in the profound silence.

Luca spun on his chair, the pain etched on his face alarming. 'How long have you been here?' he questioned, his voice low and grief-ravaged.

'Not long,' she whispered. 'I heard you play and I had to come.'

Luca looked to the closed door. 'Was I too loud?'

Gracie shook her head. 'I'm just not sleeping well.' It was almost the truth; she hadn't been before that night.

Luca pushed himself from the piano stool and joined

her on the couch. He ran a hand through his hair; it fell through his fingers and rested exactly where it began. 'It is understandable,' he finally said. 'You are so far away from home and you must be missing your friends and family.'

Gracie smiled, her voice having been stolen away by the darkness.

Luca reached out a hand and pushed a curl from her forehead, carefully tucking it behind her ear. She blinked madly.

'Something else is bothering you. Something more imminent than missing your friends. Tell me what is really wrong.'

The faraway candle lit Luca's handsome face with flickering golden warmth. His deep, dark brown eyes glowed, and glistened, and watched her face closely. His fingers, which had so recently swept across her face, lay along the back of the couch, resting by her shoulder. She ached to snuggle up to his hand like a purring cat. He wondered what was wrong with her? She wondered as much herself. But it was not only the fact that her feelings for him had her in a spin. There were more important things at stake on this night. The best angle she could come up with was honesty.

'I don't know any other way to say it than straight out. Dom told me that he is Mila's natural father.'

Luca exploded from the couch. He muttered in Italian under his breath as he paced back and forth.

'Luca, I'm sorry,' she said. 'But I couldn't rightly go on without you knowing I knew.'

He swore beneath his breath. 'My wretched brother doesn't know when to keep his mouth shut. Or his zipper...'

Had he really said that aloud? Having kept the truth a

secret for so long, Luca was shocked to find himself expressing himself so boldly.

Gracie reached out and touched his arm, the feather-light pads of her fingertips sending a shock up his bare forearm. 'I don't think you give him enough credit.'

He looked to her, knowing his eyes were wild with emotion as she flinched from him. He took a deep breath to settle his sudden rage; the rage that was all the more keen for the fact that his Gracie seemed to be sticking up for Dom. Was it happening all over again?

'And why should I give him any credit at all?' he asked.

'Maybe it's not that he doesn't know how to keep his mouth shut. Maybe it's that he knows exactly when to open it.'

What was the woman saying, talking in riddles while his heart raced so hard with the thought that she was so obviously taken by his brother? He could barely think for the blood rushing through his head. 'Meaning?' he asked, the word tearing from him.

'Meaning maybe he thought that my knowing would only make my time with Mila more meaningful. Maybe he thought it would make it easier for you to lay the responsibility you have carried on your shoulders for so many years onto someone else, if only they knew the truth.'

Luca blinked. 'No. He's not that smart.'

Gracie snapped her mouth shut and worked at her bottom lip. Luca's anger subsided as he realised she was in agony, wondering if she had done the wrong thing by telling him. The last thing he wanted to do was upset her. It was certainly not her fault that he was dealing with ancient issues. She was simply in the firing line.

He took his seat back on the couch. With the candle at her back, Gracie's hair lay in a glowing halo around her face. He had the sudden urge to take her in his arms as he had for such a brief time in the dining room. He wanted to feel her softness melt against him. To sink his face into her hair. As though that would help make everything else fade away into insignificance.

'She doesn't know, does she?' Gracie asked.

Oh, God, his little Mila. He shook his head.

'Will you...will you tell her?' she asked.

'One day.' Luca reached out and absentmindedly wrapped a tendril of her dark hair around his finger.

Gracie suddenly realised how alone they were, staring at one another by the light of a single candle. And she felt as if she was taking advantage of him. With his brother back home, he would naturally want to assert himself, to assure himself that his manhood was still viable. And there she was, offering herself to him, all wrapped up like a gift in her comfy blanket. Making him emotionally vulnerable and then taking advantage. No. Not this way.

Her yawn was only half false, as once she began to fake it a real one came right on by. 'Probably should go back to bed,' she said. 'It's been a big day.'

'Hmm.' Luca didn't seem to care one way or another as he continued to play with her hair.

She tried to extricate herself gracefully, but her blanket had wrapped itself around her and then some. She stood, it pulled her down again. She tried to kick her feet free and she only became more entangled. Within a few seconds she felt like a moth, flailing to free herself from a spider's web, only getting deeper and deeper entwined as she struggled.

'Here,' Luca said, his voice washing over her in the semi-darkness. 'Allow me.'

Gracie closed her eyes and bit her lip and tried to keep

still as Luca reached across to find the end of the blanket. As soon as she felt his breath upon her neck she flailed once more. It took for him to wrap a steel-tight arm across her for her to stop.

'Just stop struggling and I will set you free.'

Gracie looked up into his liquid brown eyes and had to stop herself from laughing aloud. In any other situation that would have been a classic one-liner, a precursor to a romantic candlelit kiss. A metaphor for the struggle she was having with her own feelings.

But she did as she was told, she closed her eyes tight as Luca tugged and twisted her until she was free of her physical entanglement. Feeling mightily embarrassed at the situation, she was off the couch the minute her feet found the floor.

'Thanks,' she said, her voice breathier than she would have liked. 'Please try to get some sleep yourself. I'm sure Dom will make it his mission to exhaust us anew tomorrow.'

'We'll see,' he said cryptically. 'Goodnight, Gracie. Sleep well.'

'You too, Luca.'

Gracie turned on her heel and ran as fast as she could with the heavy blanket trailing behind her.

CHAPTER NINE

LATER that morning she understood Luca's *we'll see* comment. Dom was gone.

'But he's coming back, right?' Gracie asked Cat over breakfast in the staff kitchen.

'I would not think so, Miss Gracie,' Cat said in stilted English. 'He only comes home to feed and shower before leaving on another adventure.'

'Does he not miss...his family?'

'I am sure he does. But I think he would miss his adventures more.'

How could he? Dom had a fairy-tale home, a loving family, a beautiful daughter... But then Gracie had had access to a brother and a sister herself, yet it was not enough. Yes, she understood Dom. One man's family was another's jail. And on the contrary, one man's jail had become another's family.

With her toast in hand, she scooted into Luca's office. This time she didn't even knock, she just entered and waited for him to finish typing. His tired eyes looked up at her and she knew she was a big part of the reason he hadn't had nearly enough sleep the night before.

Unable to look him in the eye, she continued through the office until she reached the big bay window. 'What are your plans for the day?' she asked with forced cheeriness after swallowing her last mouthful.

'What did you have in mind?'

His chair squeaked and she sensed him leaning back, watching her. She eyed him over her shoulder. 'I feel as if we have been inundated with people for days and days. How about a picnic? Just you, Mila and me. Down by that crazy creek of yours.'

Luca glanced at his tidy desk, which was devoid of its usual papers. *Good,* she thought. *He's not busy.* And the last thing he needed was to be locked away inside his office with nothing but his current thoughts to keep him company.

'Come on,' she implored. 'What if I promise not to wade into the creek fully clothed again?'

'I was actually waiting on an important phone call.'

'Can't Cat page you, or send a text message to your mobile phone when the call comes thorough? Then we can come straight back.'

He watched her through narrowed eyes then his head shook back and forth. 'I am sorry, Gracie. But this call is…sensitive. I don't want the caller to find any reason not to submit to my plan.'

What could she say? It was the middle of the week. She could hardly expect him to throw everything aside and to submit to *her* plan. But still, 'It's a beautiful day. Come on,' Gracie insisted, reaching over and taking both of his hands in hers, leaning back so that he held her weight in his grasp. 'You've been working so hard. You really deserve a break. Come and have a picnic.'

She gave a small pull but he dug in his heels.

'Gracie, I can't.' His voice came out loud and strong. He'd said no and meant it.

She let go as though burnt. She felt so stupid. Begging like that for him to spend time with her. He had tried to be polite and she just wouldn't give in. 'Sorry. I just thought… But no. Of course not.'

'Gracie, please don't look so sad.'

Gracie broke out in a big, beaming smile, though inside

her ego felt bruised. 'Sad? Me? No. I just thought you might need the break. I am totally cool bananas. Right as rain. Fine as I could be.'

Luca pushed himself from his chair and went to her. 'Gracie, I know you are not fine. I understand that pout, that down-turned mouth, those lines marking your forehead.' He reached out, running his thumb along her tightly furrowed brow.

'No, it's OK.' She backed towards the door. The last thing she wanted was for the guy to spend time with her out of pity. 'I don't want to any more. I just remembered I have something else to do too. You wait for your call and we'll just have the picnic another day.'

He glanced at his dormant telephone. 'We'll go. OK? We'll have the picnic.'

It didn't take much for her embarrassment to turn to anger. 'Luca, stop. Stay. Watch your phone. Seriously. I just thought you could use some sunshine. It's no big deal.' She knew she sounded rude, but once started she couldn't stop. She was out of control. 'I'll just go back to babysitting your kid when I could be doing something more important like combing the streets of Rome, banging on doors until I found my dad. So off you go.' She fluttered her hand at him. 'Go sit at your big, empty desk and wait for the phone to ring. Don't worry about me. I've taken care of myself thus far; I don't know why I bothered to ask for help in the first place.'

And then the phone rang.

It shut Gracie up quick smart. If this was *the* call he had been waiting for then she would look like a complete goose. If she had waited five more minutes, the picnic would have been a goer. But instead, her temper and ego had the better of her. She stared at the phone, at once thankful that it stopped her from saying anything more stupid and hating it for being such a silly cause of disagreement in the first place.

'I'll leave you to it, shall I?' she asked, her sarcasm now almost under control.

But Luca held up a hand, demanding she stay. Their conversation was not over yet. She stood in the middle of his sheepskin rug, hands wringing anxiously as she waited.

Luca answered the phone, then after a few short, clipped sentences he held out the receiver. 'It's for you.'

'For me?' Gracie asked, taken by complete surprise.

The embassy! she thought. Her heart beat so hard she could feel the pulse in her temple, though she couldn't feel her feet as she walked towards him. If it was the embassy, this would be the first time they had called her, thus this had to be it. Good news or bad. They had found her father or they hadn't. She slowed, suddenly not wanting the answer either way, suddenly thinking the hope was better than the knowledge after all.

She looked to Luca for reassurance; maybe he knew already. But his face was impassive.

She took the receiver with a shaking hand. 'Hello?'

'Gracie, is that you?' a deep masculine voice asked, and the hairs on the back of Gracie's neck stood on end.

'Yes,' she said, her voice reduced to a whisper.

'Gracie, my name is Antonio Graziano. It seems that I am your father.'

Gracie felt her legs give way, but Luca took her by the shoulders and planted her in his soft, springy office chair. Her overriding thought was that the seat was still warm from his presence.

'Gracie? Are you still there?' the man on the phone asked in heavily accented English.

She had no idea how to answer him. What to call him.

Mr Graziano? Antonio? Dad? 'I am here,' she said, still hedging her bets. 'How did you find me?'

'Your friend, Luca. He found me.'

Gracie dragged her suddenly weighted eyes up to find Luca, the man she had just accused of not caring, the man who had cared more than she could have realised. But he was gone, and she was alone in his vast office with the voice of her father.

Half an hour later the office door kicked open and Caesar came trudging in. He sat before Gracie, watching her with a big goofy expression on his face. As though sensing she needed it, he leant his chin on her lap.

'Hey, boy,' she said, rubbing behind his ear. His tail thumped against the ground. She thought about how easy it was to communicate with a dog. When they wanted attention they demanded it. They showed affection without boundaries. Happy—wagging tail. Sad—droopy ears. Whereas Gracie had no such simple truth to her actions. Disappointed and embarrassed—turn cruel and accusatory to someone who deserved the complete opposite.

A light rapping sound made her look up. Luca stood in the doorway, his knuckles resting against the wooden door. Caesar ran to him, licked his hand then disappeared out the door.

'May I?' Luca asked, and *he* looked sheepish. He who had done nothing wrong, and everything right. Gracie's chest felt tight and she knew it was not from embarrassment any more. Her heart was full to bursting. But what to say?

She nodded and assured him, 'You needn't have left.'

He gave her an almost imperceptible shrug. 'I thought you should be alone. I would only have been a distraction.'

If only he knew how much! With hands in his pockets, he sauntered deeper into the room, but he still looked wary, as though snakes might suddenly grow from her head. 'You needed to feel free to speak your mind.'

Gracie swallowed hard. She had some damage control to take care of. 'And I think we have established I can do that fairly well with you still in the room.'

She felt all hope was not lost when Luca's beautiful mouth kicked up at one side, creating a charming crease in his right cheek. 'Hmm,' he said, his deep voice carrying to her on a hum she felt in her bones. 'So it would seem.'

Gracie could not help but return the smile, but it soon turned into a grimace, which was hidden as she buried her face in her palms.

'Why didn't you say anything? Why didn't you stop me from saying those awful things, *especially* since they were untrue?' She peeked through her fingers to find him sitting on the couch.

'The truth?' he asked.

'Always,' she insisted.

'I wasn't sure if he would come through for you.'

Gracie felt herself shrink a size and wished the chair would open up and swallow her. Luca had only been trying to protect her. Of course he had. It was his defining quality.

'Unlike you,' she said, knowing she had to give him back some of the trust he had put in her.

He tipped his head on the side in a gallant nod. She wanted nothing more than to run to him and hug him, but she knew that, if she did, this time she would not let him go.

'He wants to meet me. Tomorrow,' she said, turning her mind back to the short, sweet conversation, her first ever with her natural father.

'I shall take you into Rome if you would like.'

'Are you sure? You have gone to so much trouble already.'

'Not at all. I would be delighted.'

'Then yes, please. I would like that,' she said. She looked to him again. 'But how did you find him? When?'

'You have many questions, I would think,' Luca suggested, his heartbreaking smile shining her way once more.

'Squillions,' she admitted.

'This may take a while. Shall I call for refreshments?' he asked.

'Need you ask?'

He smiled, then ordered the morning tea over the phone.

'Are you sure you have the time?' Gracie asked. 'Despite the recent evidence to the contrary, I do understand if you have work to do.'

Luca shook his head. 'Now that our phone call is out of the way, Gracie, I am all yours.'

Gracie leaned back in his office chair, trying to squash down the thought that she would like that even more than the promised refreshments.

Cat knocked and brought in the promised morning tea, and Mila came bundling into the room after her, hanging on to Caesar as though riding in his wake. 'Gracie, Papa,' she squealed, letting go and leaping onto the couch by her father, 'I helped Cat make the sweets and she said they were for the grown-ups but I said you would like me to eat them too.'

Mila looked to Gracie for approval.

'Of course, munchkin. You can even have first pick.'

Mila shot off the couch and grabbed a *crostata*, a shiny tart filled with ruby-red plums. 'After this, Pino wants us to take a ride on a Melbourne tram, so you can show us where you live, OK?'

And though it meant that the offer to have Luca all to herself, even if only for an afternoon, was negated, Gracie could not say no to that gorgeous face. Considering all that Luca had done in upholding his side of the bargain, what could she say but 'OK, sweetie. Today you will learn all about the sights and sounds of Melbourne'? She shot Luca a look over Mila's head. 'Another time?'

He nodded and she could have sworn that he looked as sorry for the interruption as she felt.

Early the next morning, Luca was leaning back in his office chair, achieving nothing more than staring out of the bay window, daydreaming, when Jemma's flashy blue convertible pulled up in the driveway.

His murky thoughts disrupted, he stood, stretching out tense limbs, watching as the dust settled about the car and Caesar came bounding up to Jemma, almost swamping her. She scolded the dog, waggling a finger at him, insisting he behave. Caesar's response was to slobber on her finger and it made Luca smile. Though it didn't come as naturally to her as it did to some, she certainly never gave up trying to look out for her extended family.

She was such a sweet girl. And he wondered for what must have been the thousandth time why Domenico had not gone after her instead of Sarina. He needed a nurturer, someone who would lay down boundaries. Instead, both he and Sarina had been too wild and their relationship had blown up as quickly as it had appeared, changing both their lives irrevocably.

As well as the lives of those around them, he admitted. Though he had no regrets himself, the regrets he felt for Sarina, for Dom, for his in-laws, even for Mila, were eating him up inside. He knew that the arrival of the bundle of possibility that was Gracie Lane had only highlighted the cracks in his desperately fortified world.

'Knock, knock,' Jemma said, bustling into his office with Caesar at her heels. Her face was flushed from frustration at not being able to keep the big dog at bay. 'Caesar is going to run away, or get hit by a car, or run someone over himself one of these days. You really should keep him locked up, you know.'

Luca felt oddly light-headed, as though he was seeing Jemma properly for the first time. 'No, I shouldn't.'

She heard the teasing in his voice and shot him a flat stare. It soon dissolved into a smile. 'Of course you shouldn't. Sorry.'

'What are you doing here, Jemma?'

She plonked a bottle of olive oil with its Malfi family moniker on Luca's desk. 'I thought that today I could take Mila for a ride on Pino. It's been a couple of weeks since I last did and I feel bad.'

He hadn't minded before, taking Jemma's constant attention as it was meant, one more part of making the best of the situation. But now something ate at him. The unfairness of it all. The fact that so many lives were put on hold. The last thing Jemma needed was to feel bad for the rest of her life, for something she hadn't even done.

'You don't have to come over so often, you know, Jemma.'

'It's no problem. I want to. For Mila—'

He reached out and took her hand in his and her prattle eased away to silence. 'Really,' he said. 'We are OK. I think it's time you set to looking after yourself. Find your own husband. Have your own *bambino*.'

Jemma's mouth opened but no words came out.

'It is no more your fault that Sarina is gone than it is mine. Let go.'

As though hearing it said out loud made it suddenly possible, Jemma wobbled on her feet and collapsed into the couch. After the few moments it took for her to collect herself she looked up at him, her eyes brimming with tears. 'You're right. I know you are. It's just—'

He sat down next to his sister-in-law, another person damaged by the thoughtless actions of his brother and his wife. 'I know,' he insisted gently, cutting her off. 'But it's time.'

Toughened after years of having to put on a brave face, Jemma managed to keep her emotions in check. But she did reach out and give Luca a quick hug. 'Thank you,' she whispered in his ear.

She pulled away and ran quick fingers under her eyes as she let out a self-deprecating laugh. 'Won't have much luck in finding a husband with mascara running down my face.'

Luca smiled.

'Speaking of new friends, how is your little Australian?' Jemma asked.

'Today I am taking her to Rome.' Now that it had all worked out, Luca went on to fill Jemma in on his bargain with Gracie. Today was the day that Gracie would meet her father. That meant that his part of the bargain had been fulfilled. Since her part of the bargain had been fulfilled from pretty much the moment Mila had laid eyes on her, it meant that their arrangement was rushing to an end.

'Wow,' Jemma said at the end of it all. 'It seems we are all being forced to make some pretty serious decisions right now.'

Hearing an odd tone in Jemma's voice, Luca turned back to her.

'Gracie is putting everything on the line to find her place in the world,' Jemma explained. 'I am moving on. Mila is growing up. And how about you?'

'Me?'

'Hmm. Sarina has been gone for over a year now. And what have you done to pick up the pieces of your life?'

'I think my life is fine the way it is.'

'Well, I think, while we are being honest with one another, that it is time for you to move on as well.'

Luca knew she was right. 'For Mila's sake.'

'No, Luca. For yours.'

He watched her through narrowed eyes. 'I thought you wanted me to be careful.'

'What did I know? You've been careful all your life. Be wild. Be young and free. Give yourself the chance at happiness you never hoped to find with my sister.'

What was she getting at? He had never breathed a word of Mila's parentage. Dom? He couldn't have.

Jemma said, 'Sarina *was* my only sister, Luca. She told me everything.' She leaned over and kissed him on the forehead. 'You saved her life by marrying her.'

'I think it is fairly obvious I didn't.'

Jemma shook her head, her eyes now brimming with heavy, unstoppable tears. 'She would have self-destructed a good deal earlier if it wasn't for you, for your support and your unconditional love of her Mila. Thank you for giving me my sister back for a few more years at least. Now it is my turn. Go get her, Luca. Go tell the girl how you feel. It's time to save your own life.'

'I have no clue what you mean,' he said, his voice coming out abnormally haughty. And Jemma, kindly, didn't push him any further.

*   *   *

On the wondrous day she was to finally meet her father, Gracie awoke to the sound of a woman's voice in the hallway. It took her several woozy moments to realise it was Jemma. Then she had an idea. She hauled herself upright and out of bed, she wrapped herself in a robe and raced to the top of the stairs.

'Jemma!' she called.

Jemma, exiting Luca's office and looking revoltingly bright and shiny for so early in the morning, took the stairs two at a time to meet Gracie at the top. Gracie received a kiss on each cheek and a waft of expensive perfume along with it. Yep. Jemma would do just fine.

'Do you have any plans today?' Gracie asked.

'Not any more. Apart from a dinner date in town this evening, I am free. Why?'

'I was hoping I could ask a favour of you.'

'Of course.'

'I was hoping to steal you this morning so that you could perhaps help me choose an outfit.'

Jemma's eyes lit up and after flitting back down the stairs her gaze landed upon Gracie once more. 'Is there a big announcement that I should know something about?'

'Not exactly. It's just…today I meet my father for the first time and I want to make a good impression, and since the only clothes I have are fit for a backpacker, I thought perhaps I could maybe borrow a dress…or something.'

Gracie stopped to take a breath and waited for the million understandable questions that would come her way. But Jemma just grinned and said, 'Of course, Gracie! You can't meet your father in frayed jeans. Come, I will help find you an outfit.'

'Are you sure?'

'Are you kidding? You are asking a woman of Rome

if she minds playing at dressing up.' Jemma wrapped an arm through hers. 'Gracie, that is what I was born to do.'

'OK. I'll just have a quick shower and change, then I'll let Luca know where I'll be.'

Jemma's beautifully groomed eyebrows hit the roof. 'You tell him where you will be any minute of the day?'

'Of course, especially since I have to beg off tutoring Mila for the day.'

'You mean you really are nothing more than Mila's English tutor?'

Suddenly Gracie wasn't sure if Jemma was prodding her or pushing her, but maybe it was just the language barrier at work. 'That's the truth of it. Why? What else would I be?'

Jemma's eyes sparkled and Gracie had the feeling that language was no barrier in this instance. Jemma wrapped a slim arm about her shoulders and herded her towards Luca's office.

'Infinitely more,' she said, 'or so many of us hope.'

It was only once Jemma gave her a small shove at the doorway that Gracie realised she had said *hope*, not *hoped*. Gracie turned back but Jemma was already bounding up the stairs to see Mila.

When Gracie reached Luca's office she coughed and Luca looked up, his gaze wary. She wondered for a moment if she had done something to displease him, then she remembered she was dressed in a bathrobe, her hair a mess, no shoes on her feet.

'Good morning, Gracie,' he finally said. His voice was low and distant and, after their experience the day before, she could not fathom why. When she had taken Mila away after morning tea she had felt as if he wanted her to stay, she had felt the separation keenly, but now he was growling at her like a bear with a sore tooth.

Under his perplexing steely gaze, she felt the need to unwrap and rewrap the tie of her bathrobe. 'Um, hi. Jemma is here. And, well, she has agreed to help me find something to wear this afternoon. When I meet my dad.'

Luca's eyes darkened even further and Gracie madly scrambled over what she had just said, what could possibly have upset him. But he wasn't looking at her, but at her hands, which were yanking hard on the ties of her robe.

'Otherwise it is this, or dirty jeans and my retired Chocoholics Anonymous T-shirt.'

'Probably best to get something new, then,' Luca agreed. 'Do you need some money?' he asked, reaching for his wallet.

Gracie flapped her hands at him madly. 'Gosh, no. Put that away. I'm sure I can just borrow something of Jemma's.'

Luca pulled out a couple of large notes. 'Gracie, please. Just in case. You can pay me back one day if you so desire.'

Gracie bit at her lip, but did not refuse the kind loan. 'Thank you. I was hoping I could leave Mila here. With you. Until I get back.'

'I have managed to keep her safe before you came along, if I remember correctly.'

Gracie bit harder at her lip. 'Of course you have. I didn't mean to intimate that you hadn't. I just hoped—'

Luca cut her off. 'I am sorry. I have…other things on my mind today. I… Mila will be fine without you. Please go. Have fun.'

'Sure. I'll try.' Gracie edged out of the office but ran smack bang into Mila, who had stormed into the office and grabbed a tight hold of her hand.

'Where is Jemma?' Gracie asked.

Mila ignored Gracie's question. 'Where are you going?' she asked, her voice distressed.

'Just out with Jemma for a little while. But your dad will still be here.'

'Stay,' Mila begged. 'I wanted to show you how well I can ride big Pino.'

Gracie peeled the little girl's fingers from her hand and gave her a little thrust in her father's direction. 'Not this morning, sweetie. But Jemma and I will be back before you know it.'

Mila sprang back to Gracie as though she were attached by a rubber band. 'No!' she shouted, her face screwing up with very real distress. Gracie looked to Luca for help.

'Mila,' Luca called, standing. 'Come here.'

But Mila would not move. In the end Luca had to take Mila into his arms, hitching her up onto his hip as the little girl collapsed into great sulking sobs.

Gracie reached out to…she knew not what. Rub Mila's back and say *there, there*? Tell the little girl not to worry as she was not going away forever? Take her from her father and stay instead? 'I don't understand what has gotten into her.'

'Maybe it is best if you go now. I'll see you back here at three.' Luca's voice was tight and low.

Gracie looked up into his haggard face. His open-book eyes were closed to her now. She nodded and left.

CHAPTER TEN

GRACIE and Jemma drove home from one of Tuscany's many hilltop towns, both shopped to exhaustion. But though Gracie was tired, and though she had a big afternoon ahead of her, she wasn't yet ready to go home.

She had not been able to get Luca's attitude or Mila's outburst out of her head all morning. There were some pretty heavy undercurrents flowing through the house, as if a storm was brewing. It would crack, suddenly, when nobody was prepared for the outcome. And Gracie had no intention of letting that happen to her favourite family. Especially when the more she thought about it, the more she realised it had a lot to do with her. She had put the household out of balance. It would be up to her to fix it. And she had come up with an idea.

She twisted on the seat, stretching out her seat belt and faced Jemma. 'I have another favour to ask.'

Jemma turned to her and laughed. 'It seems this is the day for it. What can I do for you?'

'I want you to introduce me to someone.'

'Getting people together is one of my favourite pursuits,' Jemma promised. 'Who is it you would like to meet? Some handsome Italian man to sweep you off your feet?'

Gracie felt her cheeks warm. 'Seriously, that is the last thing I want.'

'Hmm? Really? I would think any woman would want for nothing less.'

'Why aren't you married?' Gracie asked, deflecting the attention from herself.

And was surprised when Jemma laughed again. 'What is it with you two, wanting me married off and out of the picture all of a sudden?'

Gracie knew better than to ask who the other half of the *you two* could be, especially with Jemma being in such a cryptic and naughty mood.

'Anyway, it's not a man I am after,' Gracie said. This time. 'It's someone else.'

'OK,' Jemma acquiesced. 'Who would you like to meet?'

Half an hour later Gracie stood in Mila's grandparents' sitting room.

'Mama, Papa, this is my friend Gracie,' Jemma said. 'She is from Australia.'

The attractive older couple welcomed Gracie with warm smiles. 'Gracie, pleased to meet you,' Bruno Malfi said while Carla Malfi gave her a friendly nod.

'How did you two meet?' Bruno asked.

Here goes, Gracie thought. 'I am your granddaughter's English tutor.' She saw the moment the words sunk in; both expressions cooled, their smiles frozen in time.

Bruno spoke first, no longer able to look her in the eye. 'Jemma, what is the meaning of this?'

'Papa, I think it's time we stop all this nonsense. I think it's time you visited Mila again.'

'She is adorable, Mr Malfi,' Gracie interrupted. 'I have heard she looks so like Sarina. Once you set eyes on her—'

'Enough!' he shouted.

Then Jemma's mother burst into tears and fled the room.

Gracie swallowed hard. Maybe she had been wrong in coming here. No. Not wrong. She had made the hard choice. But now the ice had been broken there was no turning back. She would not give up. Especially since seeing the pain in their eyes. She knew they needed Mila as much as she needed them. As for Luca, and what he needed? That she was still working on.

Luca checked his watch for the hundredth time in ten minutes. It was after three and she still wasn't back.

He hadn't been able to get much work done all day. The remembrance of the look on Gracie's face at Mila's earlier distress had made him feel as if a steel band were squeezing his chest. He had done nothing to tell her as much, he had just sent her away.

He spun different solutions to his worries through his mind, and the one that kept coming to the surface was that maybe she could stay. For another few weeks. While she got to know her father from a safe distance. At least until Mila started school. He felt the weight lift from his chest at the thought. He would suggest it as soon as possible, and everything could stay the way it was.

'Luca?' Gracie's voice came to him softly through the open doorway.

He spun on his heel to find her standing in the doorway, blocking the light.

She wore a red dress; the soft sleeves brushed her elbows and the skirt stopped just on her knees, its exquisite fabric hugging her curves lovingly. She wore sheer stockings and red high heels. She looked like a million bucks. Like a modern-day Snow White. And as if she had stepped out of his very dreams.

'What do you think?' she asked, her usually invulnerable voice wavering uncertainly. 'Is it too much?'

He walked towards her, his feet coming to their senses before any other part of his anatomy. When he reached her, he took her by the hands, spreading her arms so he could have a good look at her. Her hair had been trimmed and styled and Jemma must have encouraged a little light make-up. Mascara darkened her deep blue eyes, rouge highlighted her soft cheeks and deep red lipstick made her mouth look ready to be kissed, and kissed, and kissed.

Too much? he thought. *If this was too much, he would put in a standing order for it right now.* He shook his head. 'You look almost perfect.'

Her face broke out in the sweetest of smiles, and Luca's warm and fuzzy mood slammed off kilter so suddenly he had to let go of her hand to brace himself against the doorframe. Who was he kidding? He didn't want her to stay until Mila left for school. And he didn't want things to continue as they had. He wanted a heck of a lot more on both counts.

'Almost?' she asked.

'Mmm,' he said, sauntering towards her. 'Something is missing.' As he reached Gracie and took her by the hand, he could feel her trembling. The poor thing was nervous about meeting her father. His excuse was less ingenuous.

'I think this will finish off your new outfit nicely,' Luca said as he looped an antique silver watch around her wrist. It hung loosely around her thin arm.

'What's this for?' she asked.

'It was my mother's. It hasn't worked for years. But when in Rome I had it serviced. I thought you would be able to give it a new life. As today, your new life begins.'

She stared at the glittering band, her throat choked. 'Thank you, Luca. It is perfect,' she said, her sweet voice liquefying his limbs. 'If you are ready, we should get going.'

Get going? The last thing he wanted to do was go! Luca wanted to take her by her trembling hand, throw her over his shoulder and storm up to his waiting bedroom. He wanted to peel that scrumptious dress from her, ever so slowly, and to revel in the even more scrumptious body beneath. And he wanted to worship her all night.

But she had other needs.

'Of course,' he said, allowing himself a small touch in tucking her hand into the crook of his arm. 'It's time for you to meet your father.'

They stood outside the ramshackle building. The dustbins had been cleared away and the front door was fixed, leaving the place looking quaint rather than downtrodden. All Gracie could think was that her Trevi Fountain wish number one had come true; she had returned to Rome. And in another few seconds wish number two would as well. She owed Neptune big time.

'He is not as ready as I would have hoped,' Luca admitted.

'What do you mean, ready?' Gracie watched as a tendril of embarrassment curled its way around Luca's face.

He took her by the hands and turned her to face him. 'I know how much this means to you. But it concerns me to see how much of your happiness you have placed into this moment. How you gave up your job, and your home, to fly halfway around the world with the only goal to find this man.'

Gracie swallowed.

'And Gracie, though in my meetings with him I have found him to be a good man, he is *only* a man. Don't rest everything you are into how this day goes. It may be wonderful, it may fall flat. But I want you to know that I believe that you are strong, and enchanting, and magnificent whether or not he is in your life.'

Not caring what he would think, that he might read into the movement all that she put into it, Gracie threw herself into his arms. He reached around until his hand was buried in her hair. And, as she had known she would, she felt warm and safe.

'Thank you, Luca,' she mumbled against his broad, comforting chest. 'You have gone above and beyond the call of duty.'

'No, *bella*. I have not nearly begun to show you how much I appreciate you.'

Gracie knew if her father had even a tenth of the charm Luca possessed, she did not see how her mother could ever have denied herself the chance to be with him. And before she knew it, she found she had begun to forgive her mother for the tangled mess her life had been. She had not even laid eyes on her father, yet her heart had begun to mend. And it was all thanks to the man in her arms.

'Come in with me, please,' she asked, pulling away so she could look into his eyes, no longer caring if he read anything there he liked.

'Are you sure?' he asked. 'Is this not a moment you wish to experience on your own?'

Her throat tight with emotion, she reached out and took him by the hand. He squeezed her hand back.

'All right, then,' he said. 'Come and I will introduce you to my new friend Antonio.'

Gracie followed Luca upstairs, keeping a tight grip on his hand all the while. When they reached the apartment, Luca knocked. She heard shuffling from inside the apartment and was so anxious she thought she might faint.

The door swung open and Gracie set eyes on the man she had come to Rome to find. In a blinding flash she remembered those moments when she had caught her mother looking at her with hastily hidden regret. Now, as she looked at the man in the doorway with his dark curls and deep blue eyes, she knew why. Those characteristics of his were so very like her own. He looked different from how she imagined: older, smaller, swarthier and sadder, but the resemblance was unmistakable. This man was her father.

'Dad?' she queried, her voice sounding a million miles away.

'Gracie,' he returned, his voice quavering with emotion. 'My heart. You have no idea how happy I am that you have come home to me.'

Luca let go of her hand the moment she gave in and fell into her father's quaking embrace.

A few hours later, as Luca's driver drove them home through the coming darkness, Gracie leant her head against Luca and he wrapped an arm along her shoulders.

Myriad conversation topics flitted through her brain. The fact that her father knew about her. Had proposed to her mother. Had fallen asleep one night with her mother warm in his arms, and awoken the next morning alone. Had left law school, prepared to follow her, until he received a telegram telling him that she had lost the baby after arriving home and was so distressed that she never wanted to see him again.

Yet even though she had lied to him, he felt none of her mother's bitterness. He knew, after all those years, that she had done it all for him. So that he would finish law school and have the life he had been meant to have. Instead he had remained in Rome, having never gotten over her.

'Was it all you thought it would be?' Luca asked, his breath tickling the top of her hair.

'Yes and no.'

'Tell me,' he insisted quietly.

Gracie yawned, her happy, tired body raking in the great need for oxygen. 'I liked him, and that's a good place to start.'

Though she had never really thought past that one moment where she looked her father in the face, she now knew she had barely begun to find what she was looking for. The journey to find her father, which had seemed like the end zone, the jackpot, now felt like merely the beginning of the journey.

'So what next?' Luca asked.

'Next there is a long trip home.' Settled as she was against Luca's warm, enveloping body, sleep came easily to her.

Gracie woke again a couple of hours later as the car slowed to a stop outside Villa Siracusa.

'Gracie, we are home,' Luca whispered against her hair, and as she dragged herself from her heavy slumber she was sure he had rested his lips upon her crown for a moment. She revelled in the idea for a few moments before stretching herself until she was fully alert.

'I'm bushed,' Gracie admitted, the heavy quiet of the night making her whisper. 'I was going to say goodnight to Mila then head off to bed, if that's OK?' Gracie had not seen Mila since leaving her sulking and sobbing in Luca's arms earlier. She had some pretty high fences to mend before she went to bed.

'Of course,' he said, his voice soft and low, matching her own.

Feeling Luca's eyes warming her back, Gracie slipped out of the car and up the stairs. She didn't stop until she reached Mila's room.

Cat was sitting in a rocking-chair, reading, while Mila played on the floor. Cat looked up as Gracie entered, then with a quick nod left the two of them alone.

She stifled a yawn and sat on Mila's bed. 'How was dinner with your *gran-nonna*?'

'*Il pranzo era buono, grazie,*' Mila allowed, but her eyes never once left Pino.

'I'm sorry?' Gracie said. Though she knew very well Mila had said dinner was good, she wanted her to say it in English.

But Mila merely said the words again, this time slower and louder. '*Il…pranzo…era…buono…grazie.*'

'No more learning for you, eh?' Gracie asked, pandering to Mila's innate intelligence.

Mila just shrugged.

'Well, how about I leave you with Pino for a little while, and when you are ready to find out what a Bunyip is, you can come and find me.'

Gracie saw interest spark in Mila's eyes but the young girl fought to squash it down. Gracie took a few slow paces towards the door when a soft, sweet voice called out, 'Gracie?'

She turned. 'Yes?'

'Can you tuck me into bed?'

'I would love to,' Gracie said cheerily, walking back into the room and going through the motions of undressing and dressing Mila and tucking her into her big, frilly pink bed.

Though Gracie had done the same for a number of nights, there was a certain preciousness about her movements. Whether it was because Gracie's mind was awakening to the thought of family, or whether it was because she felt as though these could be her last moments with Mila, she was not sure.

'You know how Mama is in heaven?' Mila asked, as though their original conversation from days before had never stopped.

'Mm-hmm.'

'Does that mean that you are my new mother?'

Gracie stopped tucking, her whole body stiff with trepidation. This was a time to tread carefully. She slowly sat down on the edge of the bed.

'What makes you think you need a new mother?' Gracie asked.

Mila didn't seem ready to answer that question so took a slightly different tangent. 'I thought for a while perhaps Zia Jemma would be my new mother, but Papa assured me she would not.'

'Don't you think you and your *papa* make a pretty good team on your own?'

'I guess.'

'Well, there's your answer. Not all families are made up of a mother, a father and a little girl.'

Mila blinked, listening hard.

'Some families have grandmothers and uncles—'

'I do!' Mila squealed, bundled along with the excitement of the idea.

Gracie patted her curls softly, trying to calm her back into sleep mode. 'You do. And so long as a family has love, the mix of people does not matter at all.'

'Do you not love me and Papa?'

Trust a kid to get straight to the point. 'I love *you* very much, Mila. And I hope to be friends with you for the rest of my life.'

'But you really are going to leave us soon, aren't you?'

Clever little chook. She fought to find a wishy-washy answer that would answer Mila's question truthfully without hurting her feelings.

'One day,' she said. Then as Mila's bottom lip quivered, she said, 'Who knows, maybe you will leave me first? You are getting bigger every day. Maybe you will already be at school by the time I leave.'

'You think?' Mila asked, puffing out her chest.

Gracie knew she would have to spend more than one

afternoon with her own father before any real connection could be made. The possibility rose that perhaps she *would* be in the area longer than she had originally planned. The thought took root so rapidly it stunned her.

'I think anything is possible,' she said.

'OK. Now Pino wants to talk about something else,' Mila said, grabbing her beloved palomino pony.

'How about a bedtime story? A favourite of Australian children. This one is called *The Magic Pudding*.'

'Is it about a...Bunyip?'

'As a matter of fact, it is...'

Luca backed away from Mila's bedroom door to lean against the wall.

He had no idea that Mila and Gracie discussed such matters. Mila had never asked him about Sarina so directly.

He didn't know whether to feel angry that he was missing these moments, or beyond glad that he had Gracie around to guide his little girl through them. He knew the former response was only a misplaced sort of envy and the second a desperate sort of fear of how Mila would cope if...when Gracie left.

He reached a hand up and rubbed at his ribs, but he knew no amount of massage would heal this sort of hurt. There was only one cure. And that would be to make Gracie one more offer she could not refuse.

After Mila fell sleep Gracie padded downstairs and, surprise, surprise, found Luca in his office.

'I thought you were going to bed,' he said.

'That was the plan, but something came up. Can I...? Do you mind if we discuss something a little sensitive?' She had to get this out before she changed her mind.

Before her own needs trampled all over those of her ward. 'Luca, I think it's time I left.'

That got his attention. He sat bolt upright, his office chair creaking noisily in its hinges. 'What? Why?'

How could she put this? 'Mila is concerned...she asked me if I was to be her new mother.'

She waited for the laughter. Or the explosion of anger. Or the deep distress that ought to come at such a suggestion, but he just watched her patiently.

'But you can't leave yet,' he said gently.

'Don't you think I know it?' Gracie said, her own mixed emotions exploding to the surface, even if Luca's wouldn't. Perhaps even *because* he was sitting there so calmly, so unaffected by such a suggestion. 'I will have to find a place in town, which I can little afford. Or I'll have to use my father's sofa, and I know it is way too early for that yet.'

'So stay,' Luca said.

'What other choice do I have?'

'Do as Mila asks.'

Gracie shook her head. 'I don't understand. What exactly are you suggesting?'

'I am suggesting you stay and become Mila's new mother. Stay, *bella*, and marry me.'

Luca knew from the look on Gracie's face that she hadn't seen his suggestion coming any more than he had. But once he had said it aloud, it felt...right.

Her throat worked. 'Luca, you don't mean that.'

He took her by the hands. 'If I didn't mean it I would not have said it.'

'Have you actually been thinking about this?' she asked, her voice a hoarse whisper.

'Well, no. But I think it is a sensible idea. We get along. We both love Mila. I think it is actually an excellent solution.'

Her cheeks warmed so fast and so pink he knew that he had shocked her. He revelled in what that choice would mean, in terms of companionship, in terms of Mila's happiness, in terms of having her all to himself, of being able to count on waking up to her warmth and beauty for the rest of his life… It took a few moments before he noticed her vehemently shaking her head.

'Listen to yourself,' she said, her voice now even though her chest was rising and falling with such emotion Luca took in a big, deep breath in empathy. 'You *suggest* we marry as it would be an excellent *solution*? Be serious.'

'I am.'

'Luca, you have already had one marriage for the sake of your child,' she swallowed, 'and you can't possibly want to go there again.'

'My marriage with Sarina was fine.'

But as he said it he knew it wasn't true, because the way he cared for the woman before him was nothing like the way he had ever cared for any woman. He cared that she was happy. He cared that she was safe. He cared that she had everything she wanted and needed.

But more than anything, he cared if she cared for him or not. No matter how perfect the idea, he could not marry this woman without her caring as strongly for him as he did for her. It would only slowly but surely break the heart that Sarina had only managed to bruise.

'You are right,' he managed to say, though it felt nowhere near as right as his proposal had felt, irregular though it had been. 'It was wrong of me to make such an unprovoked suggestion. I am sorry to have put you in such an uncomfortable situation so as to have to deny me. But, please, don't go. I will sort it out with Mila. I have been leaving her education in your hands alone this past week, and I know you have spoken of things other than English words.'

Gracie blushed and he had to stop himself from taking the step towards her, putting her beautiful face in reach of his cooling hands.

'I am so sorry,' she said. 'But she asked, and I couldn't palm her off. I had to say something and all I could do was tell her what I felt in my heart—'

Luca shook his head. 'Gracie, please. Do not apologise. I am saying I am grateful. You have no idea how much your being here with us has helped.'

The way you have brought Mila's laughter echoing through the rooms of the house, the way you made Domenico feel welcome in his own home, the way you gave Jemma the belief that she does not need to take care of us any more.

But he couldn't say it out loud. It would only confuse her, he was sure. Being such a good person, she would surely take it on board and it would make it harder for her to go. And if that was what she needed to do…

'Then I'll stay,' she said, and Luca could have roared with relief. 'You talk to Mila,' she continued, 'and explain the way things are. I think there is more you need to sort out with her before you can even think of bringing *anyone* new into your lives.'

'You are right, as always,' Luca said with a smile, though the ache beneath his ribs felt even more pronounced than it had before their conversation.

'Along the same lines, I need to spend more time with my father before we can really think of becoming firm fixtures in each other's lives. Can we continue as we were?'

'Of course,' he replied, ready to agree to anything she asked, so long as it meant that he had not frightened her away. Luca knew that the idea of things continuing as they were was pretty special in itself. He could not remember a time when he had not felt as he did for her in that moment. Impressed, enamoured and involved. 'We will go along as we were.'

She looked upon him for a few more heady seconds, her gaze so concentrated and raw. Then she took him by the face, afforded him one swift, soft kiss upon the corner of his mouth, uncurled herself from his grip and left.

Only years of practice meant that Gracie managed to put one foot in front of the other on the way to her bedroom. Once there she lay in bed, staring at the canopy with the words *stay and marry me* haunting her for hours and hours.

She'd been the one to shoot the idea down in flames, but the problem was, she was undeniably, wretchedly, deeply in love with the man. She loved his protective aura, his strong arms, his warm smile. And she even loved him for asking her to marry him, all for the sake of his little girl.

But what could she do? Especially since for the first time in as long as she could remember she wished she had her mother by her to help her through the bitter-sweet pain those words had wrought.

As surely only her mother would understand why she'd had to say no.

CHAPTER ELEVEN

IT WAS too long to wait until Saturday Night Cocktails to get the advice she needed from her girls. Later that night, once the sun had risen in Melbourne, Gracie snuck downstairs to Luca's office.

'Be at home. Be at home,' she whispered down the phone line.

'Adam speaking,' a warm, familiar Aussie voice came down the line and Gracie's relief was palpable.

'Adam, it's Gracie.'

'Gracie! How the heck are you? Where the heck are you?'

'I'm fine. Never been better. Still far, far away. Look, could you grab Cara for me?'

'Of course. Happy trails!'

Adam put her on hold, and she had to listen to advertising for Adam's company—Revolution Wireless and its new range of mobile phones. It made her smile; the guy couldn't stop marketing even at home! And it also gave her a huge pang of homesickness.

'Gracie, tell me that's really you!' Cara finally squealed down the phone.

'Please tell Adam I don't need a new mobile phone.'

There was a pause and Cara sucked in air through her teeth. 'He's put those rotten ads back on our call-waiting, hasn't he? I'll kill him.'

Gracie slumped back in Luca's chair feeling as if she were just around the corner, not on the other side of the world.

'Wait a sec,' Cara gushed, her anger with Adam gone sooner than it had arrived. 'I'll conference in Kelly.'

Gracie held on, happy to lie back and wait for her other best mate to patch into the conversation.

'Hello?' Kelly said after a few moments of silence.

'Kell, guess who I have on the other line?'

'Howdy, stranger,' Gracie said and held the phone away from her ear, prepared for the onslaught to come.

'Oh, my God! Gracie Lane,' Kelly burst forth. 'Don't you ever go a week without talking to one of us again. We have been freaking out over here! Simon will tell you I have had his bag packed twice ready to come over and find you. If it wasn't for Brodie I would be there already!'

'Hi to you too, Kell-Belle.' Gracie knew just how to deflect Kelly's ire. 'How is your gorgeous baby boy?'

Kelly deflated. 'Wriggly. Demanding. Adorable.'

'He smells like biscuit,' Cara whispered.

'He does not!' Kelly yelled. 'Well, OK, he does a bit. Now don't change the subject, young Gracie. Tell me you finally saw the Trevi Fountain, please.'

'I did.' Though it felt as if it had happened a lifetime ago. 'It was gorgeous.'

'And tell me you threw in a coin, please!'

'I did. Two coins, actually.'

'What's the second for again?' Kelly asked. 'Isn't it to make a wish?'

'No,' Cara scoffed, 'the second coin means you will marry an Italian.'

'Oh,' Kelly cooed, 'what if you *wished* to marry an Italian? Double whammy!'

'Ah, guys,' Gracie said, 'sorry to butt in—'

'Sorry, sweetheart!' Kelly interrupted. 'I am just so thrilled to hear from you. You've flummoxed me into general hyperactivity. Now, tell us, how are you holding up out there on your own?'

'Actually I'm not on my own.'

Kelly's voice came back to her deep and suggestive. 'You're not? How intriguing.'

'Guys, I know it has been a while between drinks, but can you put on your Saturday Night Cocktails hats?'

'Can we?' Cara said. 'God, yes! After living with a guy who believes Saturday nights are meant for watching or playing a game of baseball, football, pool, darts, you name it, this old gal is itching for a good girly talk.'

'Sure,' Kelly agreed. 'Consider it an honorary Saturday Night. Oh, my God! You've met a man, haven't you?'

'Well, yes…'

'I knew it!' Kelly continued. 'Some tall, dark, handsome Roman-god type, right?'

'But not how you think. I moved out of the hostel a few days ago and am now staying in his villa in Tuscany, tutoring his four-year-old daughter in English.'

The silence was deafening.

'I am actually pretty darned good at it, I'll have you know.'

'Of course you are,' her friends agreed in tandem.

Cara cleared her throat. 'But what does the guy's wife think of the fact that you are into her man?'

'His wife passed away a year ago,' Gracie explained.

'Ooh,' Kelly said, 'he's a widower? Oh, Gracie, you are such a sweet, sweet honey-bunny.'

'He's available,' Cara said. 'He's a tall, dark and handsome Roman-god type. I for one don't see the problem.'

'Me neither,' Kelly stated.

'I need you guys to give me some options on how to extricate myself neatly,' Gracie said, ignoring their last comments.

'Extricate yourself from what exactly?'

Something warm, tender and comforting. As well as something burning, intimate and devastating. And so very heavy Gracie felt as if she was about to be crushed by its encroaching weight.

'He proposed to me,' Gracie said and squeezed her eyes shut tight as she waited for their response, their laughter, their jokes that this was nothing new.

'Oh, Gracie, that's wonderful!' Kelly managed to eke out in between sudden sniffles.

'The second coin is to marry an Italian, I knew it!' Cara blurted.

'Guys, the second coin is just your basic, regular, run-of-the-mill wish, OK?' Gracie shouted, then bit her lip so she wouldn't wake the rest of the household. 'And I did *not* wish to marry an Italian. It's anything but wonderful. He only sees me as a mother for his daughter.'

'Gracie,' Kelly said. 'You know I love you so don't take this the wrong way, but I don't think any man would look at you and think "mushy motherly type". I would put money on the fact he proposed for more intimate reasons. I bet it was love at first sight. The poor guy would never have met anyone like you before and was a goner from the moment you blasted into his stratosphere.'

'You don't even know him,' Gracie said, holding her friend at bay.

'No, my sweet, but I do know you. And though it happened almost every night at work, you never called us in the middle of the night before to tell us some guy had proposed to you. That in itself tells me that this one is different from your regular oil barons and visiting dignitaries in the casino.'

'Nup,' Gracie decided, pulling out all the stops to sway

her friends. 'Your head is soft! I think you're high on baby fumes.'

'I too think it is the most perfect news,' Cara said, 'and I have no such ready supply of biscuit smell.'

'Does he really smell that much like biscuit?' Kelly asked, her attention diverted.

'Yes, Kell, he does. Now, Gracie, since you obviously want us to get you off the hook, and I'm sorry but we won't, why don't we change the subject? You haven't even told us how your big search ended up. Have you found your father?'

'I have. I met him for the first time today.'

'Fantastic news!' Kelly said. 'How did you find him?'

'That was all thanks to Luca.'

'Luca is the guy with the daughter and the good taste?' Cara asked.

'Mmm.'

'This Luca not only took you into his home, but he also did what no one else in the western world could do for you and he found your father?' Kelly asked.

'He did.'

'Yeah. Definitely good for nothing, this one,' Kelly joked. 'Ditch him and now!'

Gracie heard a door slam upstairs.

'OK. I'll take it under advisement. There was another reason for my calling; I was hoping one of you could patch a little money into my bank account. There's a couple of things I need to clear up.' She cringed as she told them the amount, which covered the money she owed Luca for her new clothes, and then some. But Cara and Kelly fell over themselves to help her out.

'Sell my TV and my stereo for whatever you can. I'll get the rest back to you as soon as I can.'

'Done,' Cara promised. 'You'll have the money ready in your bank account when you get up in the morning.'

'Thanks so much. Now I really have to go. Goodnight, guys. Love you lots,' Gracie said on a sigh before hanging up the phone.

But she still had more phone calls to make, and not long before the whole household would be awake around her. First she left a voice mail message at the Australian Embassy to let them know she would not be available for their party. Next, she picked up the phone and dialled the phone number of the airline.

The next morning, Luca watched Gracie head out to his car. She was dressed in another new outfit; this one was a white peasant top that kept slipping off one shoulder, a wide leather belt, white trousers and pink ballet shoes. She looked simply adorable.

Caesar followed her out to the car, and, while the day before Jemma had unsuccessfully chastised the big, goofy dog, Gracie crouched down to his level and chatted to him for as long as it took for him to sit. Still. Calm. Obedient.

Luca shook his head. The woman just had a way with people. With animals. With kids. She just had a way about her. He waited for her to look his way, he even had his hand ready to wave, but she hopped into the car and drove away.

He was procrastinating. Upstairs there was one girl who he had to talk to. He took a deep, fortifying breath and walked up to her bedroom.

'Hello, Papa!'

'Morning, sweetheart.'

'Gracie has gone to visit her *papa*, but she will be home soon,' Mila explained.

'That's nice,' he said, not surprised that his daughter's timetable was now revolving around that of their guest just as his was. 'Mila, my sweet, I was hoping we could have a little chat.'

'I have decided that Gracie is prettier than me,' Mila said, off in her own little world.

'Have you?' he asked, his joints creaking as he sat on the floor with his daughter.

She nodded. 'I do. I think it is because I love her.'

Luca stopped shuffling at once. Gracie was right. Mila was more than attached to her. She was smitten. If...no, when she left it would be one of the hardest days of Mila's life.

'Do you still love me?' Mila asked, her conversations shifting as she liked.

'Always and forever.'

'Even though I now love Gracie too?'

'Of course. You have room in that beautiful big heart of yours to love as many people as you see fit, and that does not diminish the love you feel for me, or Grannonna, or Jemma in any way.'

'Or Pino?' she asked.

'Or Pino.'

'Or Zio Dom?'

Luca paused, his heart burning as a moment suddenly opened itself up. 'Especially Zio Domenico. Because a long time ago, before you were even born, before Mama was my wife, Zio Dom and your mother loved one another as well. They loved each other so much that together they made you. Zio Dom is actually your real father.'

The words had spilled from him so fast he couldn't stop them. But then he wondered if he had done the wrong thing. If she was simply too young to understand and if it would only upset her.

After a few seconds of stillness, where her hands did not even pat Pino, she looked to him, her face open and content.

'Can I still call him Zio and you Papa? Because I think it easiest, since he is only here sometimes and you look after me all the time.'

Unable to help himself, Luca took Mila in his arms, wrapping her up so tight. 'Of course, my love. That is exactly what we always thought *easiest* as well.'

As though sensing the import of the moment, Mila stayed in his arms as long as he needed her there.

'This is a pretty flash machine,' Gracie called out as she poured out a couple of espressos in her father's kitchen.

'It's new,' he said, with pride in his voice. 'As is my lounge chair. Do you like it?'

'I do,' Gracie agreed, placing the drinks tray on the side-table and running her hand over the gleaming new fabric.

'I was able to buy it when your friend bought one of my paintings. It pulls out into a bed, so if you should ever wish to stay…'

Gracie's heart thumped hard against her ribs. Luca had bought one of her father's paintings? Rather than offer him money to improve his situation, Luca had helped her father onto his feet while allowing him to retain his dignity. It took her a moment to shake her head and smile. 'Of course. I would love to.'

'In fact I was able to buy a new bedroom suite and a new refrigerator as well. They should be installed for the next time you come to visit. I mean, of course, only if you wish to come visit again.'

'Again and again, I hope,' she promised and was rewarded when his face lit up.

She had spent the drive into Rome wondering if she had made the right decision in agreeing to continue to stay at the villa. The fact was she was absolutely, wholly, ridiculously in love with the man of the house, and he was not in love with her. How could he be? She was a straggly stranger and he was...well, he was quite simply *him*.

But seeing her father again had made her realise that her heartache and accompanying self-pity were worth-while. She simply had to impose on Luca's good graces further. She knew that Luca, darling that he was, would let her stay forever if that was what she needed. For now it would have to do.

'Gracie, you have no idea how happy this makes me. To have found you. And to know that now I have found you, you will not be disappearing before I even get the chance to know you.'

He echoed her thoughts so precisely, emotion welled up in her. Gracie reached out and placed a hand over his, and she realised it was her first real, natural act of em-pathy. She cared for this man not because she was con-ditioned to, but because he was likeable. And she knew it was all going to be all right.

Her sleeping arrangements could be worked out at a later time. She *had* to stay in Italy for as long as this untried, tenuous, precious relationship required it to be so. She had come looking for a relationship with her father, not for love. She could put up with a lot for the former. How much would be up to her.

Gracie kept a hold of her father's hand. 'We have all the time in the world.'

When Gracie arrived back at the villa after lunch she felt revived, enthused, on top of the world. She all but skipped into Luca's office, though beneath it all her heart raced in fear of how Luca would act towards her, considering their last conversation.

'I'm back!' she singsonged.

He met her with a smile so radiant all her fears just melted away.

'How did your visit go?' he asked.

'Peachy. And your chat with Mila?'

He grinned. 'Terrific.'

She slumped down onto his couch, her legs splayed out before her. 'It seems everything is going swimmingly all around.'

'Mmm.'

'Mmm,' Gracie echoed, feeling buoyed up by the fact that everything did seem to be going swimmingly. There were no tensions between them. No furtive glances. No embarrassed silences.

'Since everything is going swimmingly, peachy and terrific, how about we take that picnic you suggested the other day?' he asked. 'I think we could both use the fresh air.'

'Sure,' Gracie said, 'Why not?'

'Fantastic. You get Mila, I'll get the food and we'll meet at the back door in fifteen minutes.'

'Done.'

Gracie peeled herself from the couch and ran up the stairs two at a time. Any offer to spend time with Luca was an offer she couldn't refuse.

After eating a sumptuous meal of cold chicken and fresh salads along with an array of Italian cheeses and breads, Mila took Pino on an adventure away from the creek and through the high grass near by. She trotted in wide circles in sight of the adults, who sat in the shade, their backs against the trunk of a tree, giving them a chance to talk.

They had already gone over her meeting with her father, but Gracie had someone else's past on her mind. 'I would love to know more about Mila's mother,' Gracie said, her voice soft and undemanding.

'Ah. You wish to compare my rash foolishness of last night with my first botched proposal,' he said.

Gracie's mouth plopped open and then she buried her rapidly reddening face in her hands. 'I can't believe you just said that!' she said, her voice muffled.

Luca laughed and peeled her hands away. 'I'm sorry. But I have faced facts. It is not my forte.'

'What, proposing marriage?'

'Mmm.'

Gracie felt the low sound knock on her feeble heart. 'One day it will be. When the time and the woman are right.' *Oh, why couldn't it be me?* her feeble heart answered back. 'As for Sarina…?'

Luca nodded and answered her first question. 'When I came back from America, to attend my father's funeral, she was already pregnant, and Dom had disappeared. There was never another option considered. I had to give the child a home, a father, a name. And Sarina, who was a wild girl who'd had her head turned by someone even wilder, was thankful.'

'It was that easy?'

Luca laughed. 'What do you think? No. It was difficult. It took some finessing. But eventually I was able to convince those most intimately involved that it was the best course of action.'

'Nobody else knew the details?' Gracie rolled her head to face Luca in time to see him shake his head.

'Not so I thought. And then Dom opened his damn mouth the other night—'

'Hey. Stop it.' Gracie reached out and slapped Luca's arm, leaving her hand resting there, taking some small joy in the touch while she could. 'Come on, who am I to judge the way your family works? I barely know my half-brother and half-sister and it is entirely my own fault. You love Mila. Mila loves you. That's the end of it.'

'Sarina was about your age now when Mila was born and she felt her youth had been stolen from her.'

Luca turned to face her so that their noses were only inches apart. Gracie's heart beat a tattoo in her chest. The quiet heat of the afternoon sun washed over her feet, creating a kind of lazy lassitude. The day felt somewhat unreal and the warmth relaxed her utterly.

She made to move her hand from Luca's arm, but he grabbed it before she got too far and pulled it against his chest until it was wrapped up tight in both of his hands. Gracie stared at it; her small, pale hand enmeshed with his tanned, piano player's fingers.

'My reasons were not so altruistic as you imagine, *bella*.' He looked back out into the distance to watch Mila leap about in the tall grass, and Gracie was able to let out a long-held breath. 'I had a bad bout of measles as a child. And in all likelihood I can never father children myself.'

Whoa. If it wasn't one thing it was another. Gracie followed his gaze to see little Mila telling Pino off for doing something not to her liking.

'It was a winning situation for all involved.'

'And now?' she asked. 'Do you still feel as if you are in the best circumstance *you* could be in at this time of your life?'

He looked at her so hard she could feel his gaze pinning her to the tree.

'Now I wonder if I did it all just for me.'

No! she wanted to shout. Luca was beating himself up for a decision made long ago, under the most trying of circumstances. But she could only swallow in response.

'What if I had forced Dom to face his responsibilities?' Luca continued. 'Would he have stayed here, taken on a serious job, made something of himself? Would he respect himself more today? What if I had left Sarina to raise Mila on her own? Would she have had to settle down so that the lure of the city, of fast cars and fast men would no longer have been an option? Would she be alive today? And Mila. If Mila had been raised by her natural parents, she would not have this weight hanging over her. This news that when she is old enough to understand it fully will surely crush her. This secret that I created for my own selfish reasons in wanting to take control, in playing lord and master by sorting out everybody's lives to suit my own desires.'

The poor guy was punishing himself for what he perceived he had done to his family. Was that why he could not allow himself to really let his feelings go? Gracie's heart missed a beat.

'Luca, you have given up a great deal,' she said, probing around the very edge of her revelation.

'I gave up nothing.'

'That's not true. You gave up the chance to find a woman to love you.' Gracie regretted the words as soon as they left her mouth but Luca merely shrugged. Because she was afraid that he would hear in her statement the knowledge that *she* loved him. As she knew he was not up to hearing it.

'And for that sacrifice I gained everything. I gained Mila.'

'And Dom gained his freedom and Sarina gained you.'

Luca shrugged. 'I guess we can look at it from a dozen different angles, but when it comes down to it I am no longer certain that it was my decision to make.'

Luca swallowed and Gracie waited for him to go on.

'My father had died that year. I had come home from school overseas for his funeral and on that day the whole mess was revealed to me. The death of one's parents does things to a child. No matter if that child is thirteen or thirty. I became the man of the house that day, and I think I took the role too seriously. I made some decisions, some demands, that might not have been the wisest choices to make in that sort of emotional mood.'

Gracie nodded. 'I know what you mean. I quit my job, let my apartment, sold my furniture, left my friends and family and came to Rome. And once there I agreed to follow some guy to his house in the country.' She moved sideways just enough to give him a light shoulder-to-shoulder bump.

Luca laughed softly and bumped her back. 'You see what I mean?'

She shot Luca a big self-deprecating smile. 'Mm-hmm. The things we kids do…'

Once the bump was over, Luca remained leaning against her, and Gracie was sure she could feel the hot blood rushing through the veins in his strong arms.

'I think you cared for your mother a great deal,' he said, his voice low and intimate.

Gracie squirmed as the magnifying glass spun her way. Luca was getting dangerously close to a topic she would not even discuss with herself; her love-hate relationship with her mother. 'That's a given, don't you think?'

'Perhaps.' He paused. 'How old are you?'

Gracie had to think what month it was. 'Twenty-six.'

Wow, she had been away too long if she had no idea what time of year it was. 'Why?'

She tossed a stone over her shoulder into the creek, the plop creating a stir in the water, and a small frog hopped disdainfully away.

As though sensing that she was distancing herself, Luca took her by the chin, forcing her to look into his beautiful brown eyes. 'You want to know why I ask?'

Drowning in his deep, dark, heavenly, solemn, melted-chocolate eyes, Gracie nodded.

'Because you cared for her so much that you did not embark on this quest of yours until she was gone. You thought it might hurt her feelings so you waited. Even though it tore you to pieces inside, for her you waited.'

'But she always thought I was a mistake.'

'Gracie, my darling, you are nobody's mistake. You are beautiful, and warm, and giving, and enchanting. I have never met anyone more real than you. And I know that your mother must have seen all of those qualities in you, despite her broken heart.'

Could that be true? Gracie wondered. No matter their fights, their disagreements.

'And in her own small ways she helped you prepare for this as well. By providing you with an Italian passport. By putting your natural father's name on your birth certificate. Just because she and he could not go the extra mile for each other does not mean she didn't go the extra mile for you. You loved her very deeply and you have not let yourself grieve for her as you think she deserves.'

And she had loved her mother. Of course she had. That was the whole bloody problem! Luca's face wavered before Gracie's eyes.

'*Bella,*' he sighed. He moved his hand so that his thumb

could wipe under both her eyes, and it came away wet with tears.

Gracie tasted the salty warmth in her mouth and realised she was crying. The warm, slow tears turned into great, racking, heaving sobs as all of the emotion she had been keeping locked up so tight came rushing from her. The loss of her mother, the knowledge that she barely knew her sister and brother, the finding of her father, her adoration of Mila, and falling, falling, falling for Luca. It was all too much.

Luca pulled her into his arms, rocking her, his heart suddenly, finally bursting. He wished he could do more than hold her; he wanted to sweep away her pain, taking it upon himself instead.

She pulled away, and gave a great big sniff. Her mascara had run down her face, pooling in sad little puddles under her eyes. Her freckles stood out more than ever on her pale skin. Her wide blue eyes spoke so much, brimming as they were with even more unshed tears. She looked more beautiful than ever.

Gracie blinked slowly and the last of her tears spilled over her thick dark lashes and travelled slowly, miserably down her face, carrying a light trail of mascara with them.

It didn't matter that half the time she looked at him as if he was the devil himself, like she was petrified he was going to do to her what her father had done to her mother. It was an ever-evolving sequence. Their mutual attraction had been there from the moment they clapped eyes on one another by the fountain. Surrounded by all the noise, and hustle and bustle, they had found one another fascinating from the start. Her increasing fascination with him, made all the more obvious by her dread of it, only fuelled his absorption with her.

But the thing was, he was nothing like her father, and

he had never met her mother, but he would have bet his home on the fact that there had never been a woman like Gracie; a woman so warm, natural and giving. A woman with skin like porcelain, hair like silk and a mouth built to be kissed.

Luca felt his pulse racing. The blood in his head throbbed harder and faster as he lowered his head, following the inescapable path to Gracie's waiting mouth. He closed his eyes on a sigh as he leant those last few inches and then as he could no longer bear it he closed the distance entirely. And finally, after so many nights of dreaming the same, his warm lips met hers, which were wet and swollen from her recent tears.

Gracie could hold herself back no longer. He was gorgeous. He was damaged. And he was kissing her as if she was so precious she would break in his arms.

Wanting more, Gracie pressed herself against him, her arm swept around Luca's neck, tucking beneath his curling hair, which tickled her fingers, sending shivers through her whole body.

Luca gathered her to him and she sank into the kiss, becoming instantly pliant in his tender arms, allowing him to set the pace; slow, deep and burning with such heat her limbs felt as if they were on fire.

The sounds of the woods dropped away until all she knew was the touch of his mouth, and the sound of her own heart, which beat in a strong, heady thanks that she was giving in to the plea it had been making to her every day since meeting him.

Gracie gave all of herself, all of her longing, her hunger, her pain, her tears to that kiss. And she felt it all returned to her in kind. Luca gave her such tenderness, such heat, such knowledge that her whole body melted away onto another plane of existence.

Coming up for air, Luca whispered against her ear, creating an army of goose-pimples travelling across her skin. *'Gracie, mia cara,'* he said.

Then Gracie stiffened.

It was the Italian that did it for her. She slammed back down to earth as the situation made itself clear. She was wrapped in the arms of a tempting Italian. Exactly as her mother had been twenty-five years before. She was there to finally sort out her mother's mistake. Not to repeat it! Gracie tore herself from Luca's strong embrace, leapt to her feet with the agility of a gymnast and bolted.

'What was I thinking in coming here?' Gracie shouted to the passing hedges, so angry with herself she did not care who else heard her. 'To the other side of the world. On some damned fool mission with no end point in sight.'

Luca's approaching footsteps pounded on the hard ground behind her. 'Gracie, stop.'

He reached out and took her by the arm. She shook him off and kept her fast pace back towards the house.

He took her arm again, this time calling to her with a soft, 'Gracie. *Il mio amore.* Please.'

She slowed, the energy sapping from her, though her breathing remained ragged, with shock, with exercise and with desire. She waited for him to round about in front of her, but it took for him to place a finger beneath her chin and lift her face before she could meet his eyes.

'Gracie, please don't flee from this.'

'From what?' The words tore from her.

She saw the confusion wrench across his face as he searched for the right words. And her heart stopped spiraling and slipped quietly to the floor of her chest. If he knew the answer, he would have found the words without having to search so hard.

The look he gave her was so chaotic she felt the backs

of her eyes prick with tears. God, what was she doing, becoming so emotional? She was falling apart. This wasn't meant to happen.

'Gracie, there is something undeniable between us. Something warm and good. I have been racking my brains trying to find a reason to deny it, to lay the decision upon the memory of Sarina, on Mila's development, but that is all, as you say, smoke and mirrors.'

Gracie pulled away so that there was daylight between them, her arm held out straight in front of her, her hand clasped between his palms.

'The bare fact is,' she said, 'there is nothing more important to you than Mila. Certainly not…this.' She flapped a hand between them, indicating the matching beat of their hearts.

'Gracie, I understand that I did not handle the situation last night with the most finesse.' He stroked the inside of her palm with his thumb, trying to calm her, but instead it made her so crazy for him she thought she might faint. 'You might have realised by now that I don't handle myself to my utmost potential in emotional situations. And last night—'

'Papa!' a loud voice called out from behind Luca. They turned to find Mila bounding towards them.

Luca turned and swore. Gracie slid her hand from his.

'Luca, please. I have to go. Now. I'm sorry.'

Gracie backed away and left Luca to look after his daughter as she walked towards the house, more determined than ever to deny what she had found and return to searching for what she had been looking for.

Petrified that it could be one and the same thing.

Love.

And that she had found it in the one place in which she

could not accept it. Not if she was going to keep true to her promise to herself. To seek her mother's forgiveness for years of misunderstanding. It was not too late. Of that she was sure.

CHAPTER TWELVE

THE next morning Luca went into the rustic breakfast nook to find Cat and the other staff eating alone. They stood as he entered but he bade them sit down. 'I haven't seen Gracie this morning. I thought perhaps she might be eating with you.'

'Not today. She has gone.'

Luca felt his stomach drop to his knees. 'Where is she?'

'She went to the airport.'

'What?'

His voice came out so loud, poor Cat flinched. Luca took a calming breath and held out a hand to soothe her. 'When did she go?'

'Early this morning. Before it was light. She came down for a glass of juice. Gave me a quick hug then left.'

Her *'I have to go'* from the afternoon before had rung with a certain finality, a certain wrenching tenderness that had haunted him through the night. And though he had not been able to put his finger on its meaning, he had not thought she had meant to leave. He hadn't near finished trying to convince her to stay.

For Mila's sake. And, goddamnit, for his own sake!

'How?' Luca asked. 'Did she take a car?'

'A taxi was awaiting her, I believe,' Cat said.

Luca had heard enough. He was halfway out the door by the time Cat had finished talking. 'Watch Mila for me,' he said, spinning on his heel at the door. 'I'll be back as soon as I can.'

Luca hotfooted it to his study to grab the keys for his

car, his mind whirling so fast he was acting on automatic pilot.

Gracie was gone. She had found her father. She had everything she wanted. Why was he so surprised?

Because in his heart, he had thought that she *would* stay. Forever. That she would see past his inability to express himself in words, and know by his actions that he knew she belonged in his house, with him, with his family. That he ached for her, that he adored her, that he wanted her, that he needed her. But now she was gone.

Luca was not going to let her get away. He would do whatever it took to show her what she meant to him. Not to his household or to his family, but to him.

Even if he had to fly on two planes over twenty-four hours all the way to Australia to tell her. He grabbed his passport before running out the front door, not even shutting it behind him. He sprinted to his car, opened the door, leapt into the driver's seat and shut the door.

With his keys in the ignition, he looked out the windscreen to see a taxi pulling up his driveway.

Luca gripped tight on to the steering wheel. The sound of his heavy breathing filled the car. He could not see who was in the taxi through the hazy windows. It seemed as though several heads filled the car. There was a blur of activity as the driver was paid and the occupants spilled out.

Two blond teenagers, complete strangers, hopped out of the back door. They pulled at their clothes and stood in a huddle, awaiting the person in the front seat.

Finally the taxi's front door opened and Gracie emerged. Luca's breath came out in a shuddering release. He peeled his stiff fingers from the leather-encased steering wheel, and then slowly emerged from his car.

Upon hearing him close his door, the kids turned to

him as one. And, though they were blond and lanky, he saw Gracie in their eyes. He cast them a welcoming smile, though he wanted to drag Gracie away all to himself.

Once Gracie had paid off the driver, she turned to her young cohorts, who were standing together with their luggage.

She bent from the waist to be at their eye level. He could see from this distance that she was doing her best to get them to smile. But the two young blonds flicked their gazes between her and him, walking their way. Finally she stood and turned.

And when she saw him she smiled. Actually, she beamed. And it hit him like an arrow through the heart.

He did not want ever to feel the pain at the thought of her going away for good again. Not caring who was watching, he walked to her, bundled her in his arms and hugged her so hard.

'Hey,' she said with a mixture of embarrassment, and confusion, and hope tinging her voice, 'what was that for?'

'I just wanted you to know how glad I am that you have returned to us.'

She swallowed and he knew that the confusion was clearing and now only the embarrassment and hope warred with one another. Luca knew which he wanted to win, so he turned to the others.

'I see you have brought some friends with you this time.'

She blinked, then, seeing her companions again, bustled to them, fussing and fidgeting behind them. 'This is Georgia and James. My sister and brother. I hope you don't mind but I have invited them here to stay for the next few days. I wanted them to meet my dad. And Mila. And…and you.'

Mind? He wanted to shout, *I am thrilled!*

'Of course I do not mind. I am overjoyed that you have allowed me to meet your family.' Luca held out an arm, herding the two young ones towards the house. 'Come. Let me show you to your rooms.'

Gracie spent the next few hours making her siblings feel comfortable. Making sure they were fed, awake, happy. Getting to know them.

They were good kids. Easy kids. Quiet kids. Nothing like she had been. She had always been a handful. A truant. A 'contrary little miss' was the worst thing her stepfather had ever called her and he was being nice.

Mila came in from her horse-riding lesson and she skidded to a halt as she spied the two kids, who were closer to her age than Gracie's.

'Mila, this is Georgia and James. They are my sister and brother.'

Mila did her whole squinty-eyed-serious thing as she looked them over. Whatever she saw she liked. She walked over and shook their hands by turn. 'Welcome,' she said like the lady of the house. 'Are they here alone?' she asked Gracie in an adorable stage whisper.

'They are,' Gracie agreed, whispering back.

'Where are their parents?'

Gracie looked up to find the kids looking at their toes. 'Well, our dad is home in Melbourne. And our mother is in heaven.'

Mila's serious expression fell away as her mouth dropped open in shock. 'But you never said…'

Gracie could not believe it, but it was true. In all her conversations with Mila she had never told the little girl she was in the same boat.

But she knew why.

It wasn't that she had no intention of pulling the 'my mother is gone too' card. It wasn't that she had thought Mila would not benefit from the discussion. It was that it still hurt too much to talk about it.

And if it hurt her, big, grown-up Gracie who had not had such a close relationship with her mother, imagine how these two young high-school kids must have been feeling.

Gracie brought Mila onto her hip and carried her to her bed. On the way through, she caught Georgia by the arm and made her sit with them, knowing James would follow.

'Mila's mother died in a car accident a year ago,' Gracie said. And the four of them, bound by the recent deaths of their respective mothers, began to talk. And reminisce. And laugh. And cry. For the next hour or so they compared pain and memories. Gracie thought if they only felt a fraction of the relief she felt at having shared her experience, then she had achieved what she had set out to achieve by spending the money she had borrowed from Cara and Kelly bringing her siblings over to Italy.

Mila would understand that families were all different. And Georgia and James would be able to move forward, knowing the world was bigger and brighter than their deathly quiet home. And Gracie would be able to reinstall herself in her own family.

She knew she had at long last found where she belonged. She belonged wherever it was that she was loved the most.

I let you go, Mum,' she said in her head, hoping the message would travel however many miles it needed to in order to reach her mum. *'Now please let me go too. Let me go so I can love my very own Italian as much as he deserves.'*

*   *   *

Luca awaited Gracie's return anxiously.

He stared at his computer screen but saw nothing bar her smiling face. He ached to go to her, but he knew that she was bonding with her brother and sister and he would never come between them in such a fragile moment.

Eventually she would come into his study, flop down onto his couch and talk about her day. Until then he had time. And he knew exactly how to fill it. Ignoring his laptop, he grabbed a few pieces of A4 paper and a pen as he planned to write a few letters. Most would end up on the fire, never to be read by anyone but him. But he felt the need to write them all the same.

The first was to his parents, telling them how he missed them, and how he wished they had been able to know their beautiful granddaughter. The next was to Sarina. Explaining. Apologising. And telling her of the happiness he had found, asking her to give him her blessing.

But the most important letter was the one that would be sent. It was to his brother, as he was the only one left with whom Luca could still rebuild burned bridges. It was a letter inviting him to be a real part of his family. To know that he did not need to keep running away. That whenever he was ready, his whole family would be waiting to take him in for as long as he pleased.

It felt like the hardest thing he had ever had to do. Harder than making the decision to marry Sarina in the first place. Harder than the decision to take a step back from the business he had poured so much of his youth into that he had lost Sarina in the first place. Saying hello to his brother felt harder than saying goodbye to his wife.

But in doing so, the circle of lies and pain had come full circle. With this one reconciliation, the angry breach in the Siracusa family would finally be healed.

At the thought of family, Luca realised the picture that flashed in his mind was of Mila's arms wrapped about Gracie's neck. She was his family. And today would be the day he would tell her so. Not insist. Not demand. Not with disclaimers and stipulations. But an offer of himself, and the decision would be hers to take him or leave him.

The sound of voices spilled into the house and Luca could wait no more. He eased himself from his chair, and rolled his shoulders, which were aching from a dozen different tensions. Then he realised that he did not recognise half the voices blending in a mixture of English and Italian.

He went to his bay window and peeked through the curtains to find more vehicles sitting in his driveway. There was a motorbike, a rental car and a familiar saloon car.

'Impossible,' he whispered, his voice hoarse with sudden emotion.

Luca's office door burst open and Gracie stood there. Dressed in tight jeans, rolled up above the ankles, a new white T-shirt with *Italia* emblazoned over her chest and no shoes, she looked so young, so fresh and so sheepish.

Her eyes were shining with a mix of mischief and hope. He went to her; he could not help himself. As soon as he was close enough, she reached out and tucked her hand in the crook of his arm. Where it belonged. He wanted to tell her that, in such a way that she could not question the truth of it. But the noise in the foyer became too loud to ignore, and the image of that saloon car was playing on him.

'What is going on?' he asked.

'You have some visitors.' She could barely contain her excitement.

'Since when?'

'Since I invited them. You once said to me that my friends were your friends, and I have made a few new friends in the last couple of days. A few friends I thought you might like to get to know better too.'

She slipped an arm about his waist and tugged him out of the office; he followed suit, wrapping an arm about her slim waist, relishing the feeling of having her tucked against him.

He rounded the corner to find himself confronted with Sarina's parents. Bruno and Carla Malfi who at Sarina's funeral had declared to all and sundry that they never wished to set eyes on him and his again. Yet there they were. In his home. Arms laden with food. Jemma stood behind them, her face alight with glee.

'We brought the seafood,' Bruno said. Luca could see the man's throat working and knew he was as overcome by being there as Luca was that he had come.

Luca held out a hand and took the bag from the older man's arms. 'Thanks, Bruno. That is…good of you.'

Bruno cleared his throat, nodded, and then with his wife attached to his arm he walked through the house to the lawn out back, where several other people were already scattered about a long table, which was already set and covered with mountains of food.

Luca dragged his eyes away from the unlikely sight to find Gracie watching him carefully.

'What is going on here?' he asked.

'We are having a barbie.'

'A what?'

'A good old-fashioned Aussie barbeque.'

She hooked one foot atop the other as she was wont to do. The dirty bottoms of her feet showed she had been traipsing around outside barefoot for a good while. And in that moment he knew he not only ached for her and adored her, but he also loved her.

He loved this honest, down-to-earth woman who was so different from the socialites he had found entertaining in his youth, and so different again from his poor, misguided Sarina who never even had breakfast with the family without wearing jewels and make-up.

But love her he did. With all his heart and soul. He loved her so much it made him want to laugh and cry at the same time.

She held out a hand to him, a small hand, tattooed on one wrist with a drawing of a pink horse, done by Mila that morning no doubt. He took her by the hand, revelling in the feel of her warm skin shifting over his own.

'Come,' she said, and he knew he would follow her to the ends of the earth if she asked him to. 'They will be waiting for us.'

But before he followed her to the ends of the earth, or the back garden for that matter, he had something more pressing to do. 'Let them wait,' he said.

Her brow furrowed and she cocked her head, her dark curls tumbling over one shoulder.

He pulled her away from the direction of their guests. After a moment in which she held back, something made her give in to him. She followed him back into his office.

He shut the door. He knew she knew he never shut the door. He always made himself available to Mila, to hear her laughter, to hear her cries. But what he had to say was for Gracie's ears alone.

'What's wrong?' she asked, biting at her lip.

Using the grip he still had on her hand as leverage, he tugged her into his arms. Her breath was released in a ragged sigh and he knew he had her.

'Not a thing,' he said.

He reached up and tucked a stray curl behind her ear and his hand continued the path, his thumb playing over her smooth cheek, wiping away a grain of gravel stuck there. Her eyes flickered closed and he smiled.

As though it was the most natural thing in the world, Luca moved in to kiss her. And as though it was the most natural thing in the world, she welcomed him. Their lips met, all warmth and softness. All understanding. All promises of more to come.

After several miraculous moments, Gracie pulled away and leant her forehead against Luca's heaving chest. She understood its rhythm, her own heartbeat felt just as irregular.

It was all coming together. Everything she had hoped for. Perfectly.

'It must have taken you days to organise all of this,' he said.

'Mm-hmm.'

'Thank you,' Luca said and Gracie lifted her heavy head to look into his beautiful brown eyes.

'For what?'

'For loving me enough to do this for me.'

Gracie's heart soared with the understanding that he knew. He knew how she felt and had accepted it. He was ready. Finally, he was ready.

'How did you know?' she said, her throat so tight with emotion it hurt to speak.

He placed a kiss on the end of her nose. 'You've only spent the last week showing me. I only hope that I can spend the rest of my life doing the same for you.'

Luca tugged her tighter to him and she let him, wondering why she had ever struggled against such sweet joy.

'*Il mio amore. Il mio cuore*,' he said, punctuating his exhilarating endearments with warm sweet kisses that left

Gracie feeling faint. 'Grant me more happiness than any one man could surely deserve. Stay. Stay and marry me?' And this time Gracie was left in no doubt of his intentions.

'You bet I will.' She stood on tiptoe and sealed this new bargain with the most delicious, momentous kiss of her young lifetime. When she finally broke away, her eyes shimmered from the gathering tears of perfect happiness.

It seemed the mystical Trevi Fountain had served her well. She had returned to Rome. She had found her father. And she had landed herself her very own Italian. Neptune sure had a big hug coming the next time she went to visit him.

'When?' Luca finally asked.

'When what?'

'When are you going to marry me?'

Gracie thought about it. When was she going to marry her very own big, beautiful Italian? And then it came to her. With a beaming grin she said, 'Whenever you are ready to have me. *Monday. Tuesday. Thursday. Wednesday. Friday. Sunday. Saturday.*'

Luca stared at her blankly.

'You call yourself an Italian!' she cried, waving her hands about her like the best of them. 'And yet you don't recognise a line from *The Godfather* when you hear one. I can't believe it!'

He shook his head. 'And I can't believe I am going to marry such a kook.'

'Believe it, buddy. But I have one stipulation.'

'Here we go,' he said, running his hands down her back, wiping anything so silly as a stipulation from her mind.

She managed to salvage the thought from more wanton ones. 'If you want me, you have to take my family too. And yours. All of them. This house needs people.'

She saw a wave of sadness pass over his eyes. 'I may not be able to give you children,' he said.

Gracie shrugged. 'You have already given me Mila. And I think she has proven herself lovable enough for half a dozen different parents at least. Besides,' she said, 'that shouldn't stop us from trying.'

With a growl, Luca swept Gracie into his arms once more. Only the sound of children giggling in the distance stopped him from throwing her to the couch and trying right there and then.

But then a small voice called out 'Yuck!' from the doorway.

Luca and Gracie pulled apart to find Mila walking up to them, wiping her hand across her mouth as though she had been the one kissing. Once she reached them, she wrapped herself around one of each of their legs. 'Come outside. You have to see this! Georgia is cantering! Even *I* am not allowed to canter.'

Arm in arm, they followed the little bundle of energy outside to find Gracie's little sister cantering around the dressage ring. She was smiling. James was smiling. The small group of friends and family gathered about was smiling. Gracie's heart felt radiant.

Luca let Gracie go long enough to take Mila into their protective circle, but then he leaned into her at once, as though he could not stand to be parted from her for a moment longer.

'What do you think about Gracie living here with us from now on?' Luca asked Mila.

Mila turned to him, her expression so serious Gracie had to cover her mouth with her hand. But her laughter was half in adoration and half in mortal fear that Mila might, at the last post, reject the idea out of hand.

'Will she be my new mother?' Mila's voice carried

across the green and the whole crowd stilled. Their families, including Gracie's father and half-siblings, and Luca's in-laws and *nonna*, even Giovanni from the trattoria in Rome, stopped with food halfway to their mouths, conversations forgotten mid-sentence as they awaited the answer to Mila's all-important question.

Blocking out the maddening crowd, which was there as a result of her own stubborn insistence, Gracie crouched down to meet Mila eye to eye. She took Mila's small hands in her own and said, 'I would love nothing more. But it is not only up to me. Your beautiful mother will always be your first mother. But if you will have me, I would love to be your other mother.'

Mila's serious young face broke into a huge grin as she twirled about the green lawn, yelling, 'Cool bananas!'

0505/05

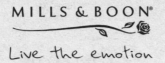

Live the emotion

Playboy Lovers

They're the most eligible bachelors around – but can they fall in love?

In June 2005, By Request brings back three favourite romances by our bestselling Mills & Boon authors

The Secretary's Seduction *by Jane Porter*
The Prospective Wife *by Kim Lawrence*
The Playboy Doctor *by Sarah Morgan*

Make sure you get hold of these passionate stories, on sale 3rd June 2005

Available at most branches of WHSmith, Tesco, ASDA, Martins, Borders, Eason, Sainsbury's and all good paperback bookshops.

www.millsandboon.co.uk

4 FREE

BOOKS AND A SURPRISE GIFT!

We would like to take this opportunity to thank you for reading this Mills & Boon® book by offering you the chance to take FOUR more specially selected titles from the Tender Romance™ series absolutely FREE! We're also making this offer to introduce you to the benefits of the Reader Service™—

- ★ FREE home delivery
- ★ FREE gifts and competitions
- ★ FREE monthly Newsletter
- ★ Exclusive Reader Service offers
- ★ Books available before they're in the shops

Accepting these FREE books and gift places you under no obligation to buy, you may cancel at any time, even after receiving your free shipment. Simply complete your details below and return the entire page to the address below. You don't even need a stamp!

YES! Please send me 4 free Tender Romance books and a surprise gift. I understand that unless you hear from me, I will receive 6 superb new titles every month for just £2.75 each, postage and packing free. I am under no obligation to purchase any books and may cancel my subscription at any time. The free books and gift will be mine to keep in any case.

N5ZED

Ms/Mrs/Miss/Mr ....Initials ....

BLOCK CAPITALS PLEASE

Surname ....

Address ....

....

....Postcode..

Send this whole page to:
UK: FREEPOST CN81, Croydon, CR9 3WZ